The Adventure of the Assassino Pazzo

A New Sherlock Holmes Mystery

Note to Readers:

Your enjoyment of this new Sherlock Holmes mystery will be enhanced by re-reading the original story that inspired this one –

The Adventure of the Red Circle.

It has been appended and may be found in the back portion of this book.

Dear Reader:

Do you want to receive notice of each New Sherlock Holmes Mystery when it is published? And hear about all free and discounted books?

Yes? Then please do any or all of the following:

Follow me on Bookbub here:

www.bookbub.com/profile/craig-stephen-copland?list=author_books

Follow "Craig Stephen Copland" and "New Sherlock Holmes Mysteries" on Facebook

Follow me on Amazon Author Central here:

amzn.to/2JOJVvt

Warm regards,

CSC

The Adventure of the Assassino Pazzo

A New Sherlock Holmes Mystery

Craig Stephen Copland

Published by:

Conservative Growth Inc.
3104 30th Avenue, Suite 427
Vernon, British Columbia, Canada
V1T 9M9

Cover design by Rita Toews

Cover image © Shutterstock used under license
1275973558

ISBN-: 9798700926768

Dedication

To the doctors, nurses, therapists, social workers, clergy and others who dedicate so many hours to the care and treatment of those who suffer from mental illness.

And to those who struggle with many afflictions that strike the mind and cause them to face and overcome hardships that those of us who have never had to deal with mental illness know so little about.

Contents

Acknowledgments

All of us who write Sherlock Holmes pastiche mysteries are obligated to express our profound gratitude to Sir Arthur Conan Doyle for his creation of Sherlock Holmes.

So, again, dear ACD, thank you.

As readers of my New Sherlock Holmes Mysteries know, every story in this series is written as a tribute to one of the sixty original stories in The Canon. The one you are about to read was inspired by *The Adventure of the Red Circle.*

Many of the chapter drafts of this story were shared with the Buenos Aires English Writers Group at our weekly online meetings. Since COVID struck, our loyal members have scattered to all corners of the earth, but once a week we gather electronically to help each other. It is a highlight of our week. My appreciation for their encouragement and friendship is duly noted. Thank you, my friends.

Members of the Vernon Writers Critique Group have also provided valued advice as I wrote this story, as did my weekly writing buddy, Geoff White.

All of my stories are reviewed by my wife, Mary Engleking, and my big brother, Dr. James Copland. Their general suggestions and copyediting are invaluable. Again, I thank my loyal beta readers who have reviewed so many of my efforts and made useful suggestions.

Special thanks goes to Cheryl Adamkiewicz for her generous provision of copy editing and to Michael Iwan, John Shepherd and Virgil Bolton for allowing me to use their names and personae in the story.

I take full responsibility for any and all historic and geographic errors. However, one of the advantages of publishing independently is the ability to correct errors almost overnight. Should readers find them, they are kindly requested to notify me and I will make the required fixes immediately.

CSC (craigstephencopland@gmail.com)

Chapter One

My Account of Holmes's Current Adventure

"What do you think of this, Holmes?" I said, disturbing his concentration.

"Of what?"

"It's the opening of my account of our current case."

"That case is far from over. How can you even think of writing about it yet?"

"Because," I said, "all of London are holding their breath, waiting for Sherlock Holmes to solve it, and I am quite certain you will succeed. So, put the monograph down and listen for a minute."

"Fine. Get on with it."

Sherlock Holmes and I were seated beside the hearth in 221B Baker Street on a miserable morning in November of 1899. Our involvement in a case that was all over the press had begun the previous afternoon. You might say it started off with a bang. What had happened already was so unusual that I could not wait to put my pencil to paper and start telling the story.

"Right. Here goes." I said.

"It was a dark and stormy day. The rain fell in buckets, and the wind swept across Hyde Park, seizing the spray from the Serpentine Waterfall, mixing it with the pounding precipitation and drowning us as we held on for dear life. (For it is in London that our scene is set). Sherlock Holmes and I were clutching any fixed object we could find to avoid being picked up and hurled into the angry sky. We were waiting, solitary in our pitiful shelter underneath the balcony of the Hyde Park Hotel, hoping against hope to trap our prey, the terrifying killer from Brooklyn, before he claimed another victim.

Then the singularly unexpected, the impossible to predict, happened. The body of an unknown woman descended from one of the floors above our heads and landed with a sickening thud directly in front of us. We had been too late. Sherlock Holmes, having been hired by Scotland Yard, shouted to me over the tempest, "Come, Watson, the game is afoot."

"Well, Holmes, how about that for a gripping account of what happened yesterday?"

"Frankly, my friend, it is absurdly sensationalist and utterly appalling in its inaccuracy. A dog pounding a typewriter could have written better."

I was crushed, but it was not the first time he had disparaged my efforts, and I was determined not to let it hinder me. I shot back.

"Very well, then, Holmes, could you do any better?"

He took out his pipe, lit it slowly and began to puff on it.

"Quite likely, I could. As you have your pencil in your hand, you should write this down."

"At precisely eighteen minutes past four o'clock on the twelfth day of November in the year 1899, Sherlock Holmes and Dr. J. Watson stood beneath the first-floor balcony on the northern wall, on the far west end of the Hyde Park Hotel. It was raining. The already-dead body of a woman fell to the pavement in front of them. Sherlock—"

"How do you know she was already dead before she fell?" I demanded.

"By the terrified, blood-curdling scream."

"There was no scream. She fell in complete silence."

"Precisely. Now, keep writing. I shall continue."

"Sherlock Holmes looked at the body and knew immediately that it was that of Madame Joyelle Routhier—"

"You never said so at the time. How did you know who she was?"

"When I know something, I do not feel the need to announce it. If you must know how I knew her name, kindly note that her abundant French perfume was *Mille Fleurs,* one of the most expensive available in Paris. The money spent on her shoes and clothes would have purchased sufficient food to feed every starving child in *Haute Volta.* The Press reported that Monsieur and Madame Routhier were visiting London and staying at the Hyde Park Hotel. Who else could it have been? Utterly logical."

"It is not logical at all," I protested. "Every rich French woman wears that perfume, and there must be a dozen of them staying in that hotel. They all stay there because it's next door to their embassy. It was impossible to know who she was just because her name was in the newspaper."

"So was her picture."

"Oh."

"Continue on, my dear Doctor, or is that all you wrote?"

"No, I have written more. This is what happened next."

"In a flash, Sherlock Holmes called for the local constable, and the two of us charged through the maelstrom to the entrance of the hotel. Holmes laid his strong hands on the arm of the manager and dragged him up the stairs—"

"We used the lift," said Holmes.

"You have no sense of drama," I said. "Let me finish."

"When we reached the top floor and the room from which the body had been tossed, Holmes shouted to me, 'Watson, kick the door open!' I was about to do so when the hotel manager produced his passkey. Lying on the floor in the middle of the splendidly furnished room was the dismembered but otherwise elegantly dressed body of the occupant. "Oh, no!" cried the manager. "It's our guest from St. Etienne, France, who checked in yesterday with his wife and ordered flowers and Champagne and demanded privacy, Monsieur Danton Routhier."

"Ah ha!" I ejaculated. "That madman from Milan, the crazed killer from Campania, the lunatic from Lombardy, the insane escapee from Broadmoor, the infamous Gaetano Gorgiano, known to all as Red Gorgiano, has struck again." We knew that the devil from America who hated the French and who had been put away two years ago had tortured and executed his next two victims and added them to a list that included a French merchant sea captain and an importer of Camembert cheese."

"There," I said, putting down my pad of paper. "I suppose you object to that as well."

"Of course, I do. You cannot write things that are false."

"What's false? You searched the room. That French chap was lying dead, and the manager knew his name and identified him."

"It is false to say that *we knew* it was the work of Gaetano Gorgiano. That was speculation, mere conjecture. We had no such certainty."

"Very well, then," I grumbled as I took my pencil and stroked out my last paragraph. I started to re-write it when Holmes interrupted.

"Watson?"

I looked over at him and noticed him checking his watch. "What is it now?"

"As you are not doing anything terribly important, I could use your help for the morning."

"Well, I suppose I could. What do you want?"

"I have an appointment at Broadmoor in three hours. I hope you are able to come with me."

"Broadmoor? What for?"

"Scotland Yard has contracted for my services, and I need to consult with the medical staff there concerning this Gorgiano chap and see what we can learn about him."

"But you just said—,"

"I said it was false to say that *we knew,* as we did not *know.* I did not say that the speculation and conjecture were without cause, despite their being trumpeted by the Press. Newspapers do occasionally get more than the date right, and they have correctly reported that four people have already been murdered. So, can you join me, or do I have to say something inane like *Come Watson, the game is afoot?*"

I shook my head, muttered to myself, got up, and fetched my Macintosh and umbrella.

Chapter Two

En Route to the Criminal Lunatic Asylum

On a good day, we would walk from Baker Street to Paddington.

This was not a good day. The equinoctial gales were still gusting through the city, and one risked appearing ridiculous whilst wrestling with an umbrella turned inside-out if one tried walking along the pavement. We found a cab and, ten minutes later, we were under the covered shelter of the station and ready to board the next train to Reading.

Once inside our cabin and on our way, Holmes sought whatever superficial knowledge I had that pertained to our visit.

"I've never," he said, "been inside the Criminal Lunatic Asylum at Broadmoor. I have read the recent reports in one of the newspapers claiming to expose the failings of the place, but they must be taken with a grain of salt. Have you been there before?"

"Oh, yes, several times. Many doctors have to. My first was during my training as a military doctor. I was surprised to learn how many of our soldiers end up in either Broadmoor or Bethlem. War is a horrible enemy of the mind as well as the body."

"But those soldiers who lose their minds are put in hospital asylums, are they not?"

"For the most part, they are," I said. "But some of them commit criminal acts, and a few are terribly violent. It did not do to put such men in Bethlem, where an unpredictably crazed fellow might be housed next to a gentle, docile soul who was merely feeble-minded. Neither did it work out well to put them in our prisons where they might have a lunatic fit and scream all night, bedeviling all those run-of-the-mill prisoners who were serving time for stealing from their employers."

"Thus, the government built Broadmoor?"

"They did," I said. "It opened almost forty years ago and has, overall, done a good job. Most of the patients—the ones you do not read about in the press—are treated effectively and within five years or so are able to go back to their friends and families and resume some semblance of a normal life."

"And are you and the others of your profession concerned that they may re-offend?"

"Not usually. A handful of the women patients are there because they killed their husbands, but the majority of them were sent away for murdering their children. Usually they do so whilst in a period of exhausting sadness shortly after giving birth and during the period of lactation. They are not likely ever to hurt anyone else, and judges and juries are prone to accept a defense of insanity rather than try them for murder."

"And the men?"

"They are sent for any number of reasons. As I said, some are soldiers having returned from the wars. Some are delusional and sincerely believe that their voices have told them to commit heinous acts. Some are old and senile but have become violent. Some have tried to kill themselves and others several times and are there for their own protection. And some are suffering from the disastrous effects on the brain of spirits or narcotics. These men are not criminals. They are ill. They are sick. With proper care and treatment, many of them recover."

"But not all."

"Sadly, that is true. Some are so broken in their minds that they can never be permitted to rejoin society."

"And are there still others?"

Here I paused and sighed. "Yes, there are others. There are those who are so utterly given over to malice that they must be incarcerated until they die. Meeting them and talking to them leaves one convinced that there is a force of evil at work in the world and that it has taken over the minds and souls of some men, and the carrying out of horrifying deeds has become their *raison d' être*. They are the ones you read about in the newspapers."

We carried on chatting until we came to Reading, where we changed trains and boarded the local line to Crowthorne. Then it was my turn to ask questions.

"As I do not *know* for certain that this Gaetano Gorgiano was involved, what can you tell me about him? For reasons of speculation only, of course."

I was attempting to be humorous, but Holmes did not smile.

"He is from New York—Brooklyn, to be precise. He came over to England for the funeral of his uncle, Black Gorgiano. You remember him, I assume?"

"The last time I saw him, he was rather dead, a result of his throat having had an unfortunate run-in with a long, sharp knife that was driven blade-deep into his body. That fellow?"

"The very one. The nephew must have liked it here in England, and he took up residence in Clerkenwell, where all the immigrants from Italy live when they first arrive. He had attended medical school briefly in New York, but whilst in England, he worked as a mason and was reported to be a diligent, competent, and responsible craftsman. Two years ago, on a Sunday, he took a train down to Dartford and waited until it was dark. Then he silently entered the estate home of Lord Devonborne. In the period of no more than an hour and without a sound, he cut the throats not only of His Lordship but also the wife, the grandmother, four children, the dog, the cat, and the youngest girl's pony."

"The work of a madman," I said. "A monster."

"That is what his barrister pleaded for him, and the judge and jury agreed. Had he only killed the adults, he would have been hanged by now. When they added in the children, it was assumed that he was at least temporarily deranged. But when the jury heard that he had killed the dog, the cat, and the pony, they concluded that he must be entirely insane as no reasonable human being, not even an American, would be capable of doing such foul deeds and still possess *mens rea*. He was sent off to Broadmoor."

"How did they catch him?"

"Lord Devonborne apparently knew that he was in danger and told several local merchants, the constable, and the stationmaster to be on the lookout for Big Red Gorgiano. Three people reported seeing him in the village but not in time to warn the estate."

"So, he planned it all quite carefully?'

"He did, and therefore, to my mind, he might not be mad, only dim-witted. But what was that argument up against a dead puppy and strangled kitten?"

"How did he escape, and why is he killing off all those rich French folks? He's already murdered three men and one woman. Why?"

"We *assume* it was he, and no one knows why. If it was, then is it is imperative that I find him and stop him before he murders any more of them. Garnering insights to help us do that is the purpose of our visit."

Chapter Three

The Doctor and the Nurse

Her Majesty's Government has dictated that the Broadmoor Criminal Lunatic Asylum is a *hospital,* not a prison, and that those treated there are patients, not criminals. This farce immediately vanishes when one approaches the vast institution. The first view of it is of several miles of high red-brick walls that make escape impossible. Visitors are inspected at the gate and must have obtained permission in advance to visit their family members who are not *imprisoned* but *receiving treatment.*

I first visited Broadmoor many years ago during my medical training. I well remember how pleased I was upon passing through the gates to see such a pleasant setting. There were acres of rolling grass-covered hills and lawns, lovely gardens, and artistically arranged shade trees. The buildings were designed by some of the country's leading architects and featured symmetrical arched windows adorned with decorative flourishes.

That enjoyable feeling was utterly destroyed when I was no more than thirty yards into the grounds. From one of the buildings, there came a long, horrible scream of pain and terror. I stopped in my tracks, and my heart started pounding.

"Merciful heavens! What are they doing to him?" I demanded of the chap beside me, who had already made several visits to Broadmoor.

"Nothing," he said.

"It cannot be nothing! That man is in excruciating pain."

"He is, yes, but he is doing it to himself. His pain comes from his memories and his hallucinations. No one is touching him. He is tortured by his mind and his soul."

It was a lesson I never forgot, and it returned in full force when Holmes and I approached the high iron gates of the main entrance. The miserable weather of the previous hours had passed, and the sun had emerged, making the entryway seem somewhat like a fairyland, with sunlight glistening from the still-wet grass and leaves.

Several burly chaps stood watch over the gate and, upon confirming that we had permission to enter, they allowed us to pass through. One of them called out to a guard, another burly young man, to come over and take charge of us.

"Good morning, Mr. Holmes, Dr. Watson," he said. "I am Virgil Robert Bolton, and I have been assigned to be your guide and guard for the day. Let me assure you that it is an honor for me to have the privilege of hosting two such illustrious visitors."

"We have," said Holmes, "an appointment with Dr. Lucheni. Kindly take us to his office."

"Follow me, please," said our guide. He set off along a paved path to an impressive-looking building to the right of the central administrative block.

"I take it," Mr. Bolton said, "that you're here about that Red Gorgiano chap. Quite the piece of work, isn't he?"

Holmes stopped walking, causing our guide to do likewise.

"My communication with Dr. Lucheni," said Holmes, "was in strictest confidence. Pray tell me how you became aware of the reason for my visit."

"Nothing to it, Mr. Holmes. When the word went around that Sherlock Holmes was paying a call on Broadmoor, no one had to ask why. We've only had one man escape in this past year, and he's been all over the press for killing off those *monsieurs*. Why else would you be coming?"

He turned and recommenced to walk along the path. Holmes did not move, causing our guide to stop and turn around and give Holmes a look that said, *Well, are you coming or not?* Holmes ignored the look and posed another question.

"As you appear to be knowledgeable concerning my visit, kindly stop for a minute and tell me what else you know about this Gorgiano fellow."

"Only what's been reported in the newspapers, sir. But if you want to know all about him, I'd suggest you not spend too much time with Dr. Lucheni."

"And why not? Gorgiano was one of his patients, wasn't he?"

"He only started working here three months ago. There were two doctors before him who looked after Big Red. That's what we all called him."

"And who were they, and where are they now?"

"Dr. Aleksy Bialkowski was the one who checked him in two years ago. He's gone to America. And Dr. Zaharia Tatarescu had him after that, but he left and went to Australia."

"Which renders them somewhat useless for my investigation. What then is it you are suggesting to me, as you are clearly attempting to give me some sort of direction?"

"Well, sir, if I were you, I might go and have a chat with Mr. Shepherd. He runs the Records and Archives Office. He knows things."

"That suggestion was useful. Thank you. I may take your advice. Now then, please lead us to Dr. Lucheni's office."

He led us on to a smaller edifice adjacent to the central building and that appeared to house the offices of the medical staff. The brass plate on the glass panel of the door at which he stopped read *Dr. Tito Lucheni.* A knock on the door was greeted by an enthusiastic "Come in!"

The office was similar to a thousand doctors' offices throughout England. One wall was lined with bookshelves and the other covered with framed diplomas and scenic photographs and paintings. The only exceptions to the standard medical retreat were the paucity of books and the presence of two desks, not one.

A relatively young man, a handsome fellow with a distinctive Mediterranean look to him, stood up behind one of the desks and walked toward us. He was tall and well-made, and his bearing had time spent in military service written all over it. As he approached me, I noticed his distinct limp. His left leg had been injured at some point in his past.

At the second desk, there was an attractive young woman who also looked as if she had come from Mediterranean climes. I did not wish to stare at her, but even a quick glance allowed me to see the family resemblance between the two of them.

"*Buongiorno,* gentlemen. Welcome!" said the doctor as he approached. "Such an honor to have the two of you visit me in my office."

He shook our hands but refrained from attempting to kiss our cheeks. He had been in England long enough, no doubt, to have learned that lesson.

"Mr. Holmes, Doctor Watson, allow me to introduce myself. I am Doctor Tito Lucheni, and this lady is my sister, Michelina. She is as qualified as I am, but because of the restrictions on women in our profession, she serves as a nurse rather than a doctor. We work together, and we are delighted to be of service to you."

His English was fluent, with only a trace of an Italian accent. On his wall, I observed diplomas in both his name and that of his sister from the *Università di Pisa,* citations from the Italian army, and photographs of scenic villages in what I assumed must be Tuscany. The miniature replicas of the Leaning Tower of Pisa that all English tourists to Italy bring back with them were blessedly absent. Rather than speaking to Holmes, he turned to me.

"Ah, *mio collega, mio fratello.* You were an army doctor, just like I was. I read that you served in Afghanistan and took one in your leg."

"I did. It was not our finest hour. And you? You were wounded as well, I can see."

"*Sì.* In Africa. Neither was it ours, but we served and did our duty, did we not? My sister also served there."

He gestured toward the lovely dark-haired woman behind the second desk.

"Michelina," he said, "and I worked together in the medical tents. But she is smarter than her big brother and avoided all the bullets that came our way."

I smiled and nodded to her, and she respectfully nodded in return.

"Perhaps," said Holmes, "the three of you could meet together later and exchange your war stories. I fear that our time is of the essence."

"Of course, of course, Signore Holmes. You have come on urgent business, and we have prepared completely for your visit. But, *per favore,* Mr. Holmes, we are from Italy, and it would be an unspeakable affront to our mother and father if we did not offer refreshments to our guests."

The woman, Nurse Michelina, stood and walked over to a credenza that ran along the wall of pictures and diplomas.

"*Lo prenderò,*" she said and removed a cloth cover from a tray and set it at the edge of her brother's desk. "Gentlemen, here is the best coffee in the world for you, and *ciambelle,* a favorite of our family. Please, enjoy, and when you are finished, you must refresh yourself with *limoncello.*"

She gave both of us a captivating smile. I allowed myself a somewhat improper thought and concluded that it was not without reason that so many Englishmen had traveled to Italy and never returned.

The rings of twisted bread were delicious, and the coffee was indeed exceptional. I would have been glad to relax and enjoy the repast, but Holmes took one bite and one sip and started up again.

"About your patient, Gaetano Gorgiano, how did he escape?"

Chapter Four

We Meet the Archivist

"When Michelina and I first came to Broadmoor," the doctor began, "we were informed by other doctors and the staff that this Gaetano fellow, who they all called Big Red or Red Pisano or Red Terrone, was never, one might say, the head of the class. They considered him a simpleton."

"And you do not?"

"He was far more clever than they gave him credit for and made of sterner stuff than they imagined. A hospital of this magnitude must be provisioned by several service wagons every day. A few weeks ago, one arrived that was bringing hospital supplies, and that would then take away waste. Waste from a hospital is not a pleasant commodity, Mr. Holmes. There is often blood and soiled linen and the like. There will be—,"

"There is no need for details. I can imagine," said Holmes. "Carry on."

"*Certo.* On that day, the wagon had a large vat that had been filled with waste. When no one was looking, Gaetano Gorgiano crawled into the vat and hid himself under all those malodorous items and stayed there for a least an hour until the wagon pulled into the yard of the company that cleans and disinfects all of our materials and supplies. Then he escaped."

"Was he that clever when you met and talked with him?"

"Very. His previous doctors were from Poland and Romania, and they could only speak to him in English. Gaetano was not fluent in proper English, only what they speak in America. So they thought him feeble-minded."

"But you," said Holmes, "were able to speak to him in his native tongue."

"Sì. Not precisely, of course. My sister and I are from the North, Milano. And we studied in Tuscany. Gaetano was from the South, Napoli. They do speak Italian there as well, but it is a much rougher dialect. Of course, we could understand everything he said, and he was far from being slow in his mind. Evil, yes, but not slow."

"Why do you say *evil*?"

"It is impossible for any sane man or woman to know what takes place inside the mind of a man like Gorgiano, Mr. Holmes. When he came from America, he appeared to be just another foreigner. But then something snapped inside his head, and he believed that he was called to destroy a man and his entire family. After he carried out that terrible deed, he was placed in this hospital, and he acted like a normal man for nearly two years. Then something else happened inside him, and he was driven by his demons to escape and then to go on a rampage against French people living in London. For what he has done, I have no other explanation than evil. Do you, Mr. Holmes?"

"I never met the man and only know what I read in the newspapers. I am not in a position to render judgment on his mind or his soul. However, I am hoping you can enlighten me as to why he became obsessed with the French."

"Something happened, Mr. Holmes. We do not know what it was. There are three men here in Broadmoor who are French. Maybe one of them offended him, or he perceived himself to have been offended. We don't know. Perhaps it was a memory of some event in his life in America before he came to England. If so, we will never know."

"Quite so. Then, pray tell me if he ever exhibited violent and vicious tendencies whilst in your hospital?"

"His actions, sir, were always controlled. His thoughts and speech were not."

"Explain, please."

"We make some use of the techniques developed in Vienna for encouraging a patient to speak about his childhood, his dreams, his innermost thoughts. Gaetano Gorgiano spoke to us of things he imagined doing to people, acts so hateful that I cannot bring myself to repeat them. He would degrade, torture, and defile his imagined victims. He seemed to take demonic pleasure in planning how he would inflict excruciating and prolonged pain. From what I have read in the veiled references in the press, it would appear that he is now carrying out those terrifying plans. Is that true?"

"It appears to be. He inflicts torture on his victims."

We talked on for several more minutes and shared a final glass of chilled *limoncello* before Holmes stood and prepared to depart. He thanked the doctor and nurse for their insights and hospitality, and we left their office. The guard, Virgil Bolton, was waiting for us.

"Do you have time," he asked us, "to visit the records office?"

Holmes took a look at his watch, and I expected he would decline and want to hurry back to London, but he gave the guard a bit of a look and agreed.

"We can spare a few minutes," he said. "Please take us there."

"It's up the top of the main building, sir. Just follow me."

We walked along far enough behind the fellow for me to whisper to Holmes.

"We don't have much time. We might miss our train. Are hospital records *that* important?"

"This chap believes they are, and he clearly wants us to see them."

We climbed up to the third floor of the central building. I was impressed with all the facilities that had been installed for treatments, recreation, worship, reading, learning, and the like. It was good to see that England had become progressively more enlightened in its treatment of those who are ill in their minds. Directional signs and arrows pointed to various departments, and upon reaching the top floor, we followed the one that identified the Hospital Records Office.

At the end of the corridor, we entered the room and found ourselves looking at rows and rows of library stacks, all filled with file folders.

"Mr. Shepherd!" shouted our guide. "You have visitors!"

A silver-haired gentleman of the same vintage and Holmes and me emerged from one of the aisles of the stacks of files. He was pulling his suit jacket on as he came toward us.

"Good morning, gentlemen," he said. "How may I assist you this morning?"

"We are only seeking some information concerning one of your patients," said Holmes. "Might we have a brief word with you?"

"If it is to be brief, happy to oblige. I am frightfully busy at the moment. A local photographer came in last week with an enormous box of photographs he had taken of the construction of the hospital forty years ago. I've been busy getting them sorted and recorded and mounted. It will be a week before I'm fully free to have a word with anyone other than my pencil and ledger. However, I will do what I can to answer your questions."

"Thank you, sir," said Holmes. "My name is Sherlock Holmes—"

"*The* Sherlock Holmes?"

"Unless there are two of me."

"Well now," he said, "it is not every day that a famous detective visits my modest office of records and archives. To what do we owe this honor?"

"Not to *what*," said Holmes, "but rather to *whom*. To be precise, to Mr. Gaetano Gorgiano."

"Ah, yes, the missing Red Gorgiano. I read in the papers that Scotland Yard had conscripted Sherlock Holmes to find our boy. Would you like to read his file? It is quite extensive, but I can find it for you and have it ready by tomorrow morning. You would be welcome to sit here and read for as long as you wish."

"Our time is pressing. Would you mind terribly stopping what you are doing for a few minutes and bringing his file out to us? I apologize for the inconvenience we are inflicting upon you."

He scowled ever so slightly but forced a smile. "I'm sure I can, Mr. Holmes. Have a seat, and I'll fetch it for you."

We sat down at a work table and waited for about ten minutes for the fellow to reappear. He returned, bearing an armload of files.

"Here you go, gentlemen," said Mr. Shepherd. "Out hospital being an institution of Her Majesty, everything you can imagine is recorded and filed away."

He set them down in front of us. There must have a dozen or more individual files, all clearly marked with the dates of events and reports contained therein. Holmes and I began with the earliest and started to peruse newspaper clippings reporting the deaths of Lord Devonborne and his family. We did not get far.

"MISTER SHERLOCK HOLMES!?" a voice bellowed from somewhere in the hall outside the office.

A uniformed constable entered the room. "Mister Sherlock Holmes?"

"I am he," said Holmes. "Why are you looking for me?"

The officer walked quickly over to where we were sitting. "Constable Garwin Tenney, Crowthorne Constabulary Office, sir. Sorry to have to break up your meeting, sir. But we had an urgent wire from Scotland Yard telling us to find you and get you on a train back to London on the double. Would you mind coming with me, sir?"

"Not at all. Do you know why I have been sent for?"

"This telegram is for you, Mr. Holmes."

He handed Holmes a telegram slip, and he handed it on to me. It ran:

HOLMES. REPORT TO SCOTLAND YARD STRAIGHT AWAY. GORGIANO HAS STRUCK AGAIN. LESTRADE.

"Mr. Shepherd," said Holmes, "it appears that I have to leave immediately. Would it be possible for you to let me take these files with me?"

"I would if I could, but I cannot. Her Majesty has decreed that the files are highly confidential and cannot be removed from this room by anyone who is not on the staff of the hospital. Even our doctors can only take the files away for two days at most."

Holmes checked his watch and scowled.

"Surely, sir, you know of the urgency in finding this Gorgiano man. It is imperative that he be returned here as quickly as possible, and his files could prove to be useful to that end."

"By the look on your face whilst reading that note, I assume that he has already struck again, and we need to get him back here before he does horrible things to any more French folks who happen to be in London."

"Precisely."

"Then I have just the solution."

"And what might that be."

"You are not permitted to take the files off the premises, but I am. Therefore, allow me to suggest that I will bundle up all of Mr. Gorgiano's files, re-read them this evening, and appear at your door in London tomorrow morning. I will return here by the late afternoon, and I doubt that anyone will notice that either I or the files were gone all day. Might that suffice for your needs, Mr. Holmes?"

Holmes smiled and nodded. "Brilliant, my good man. I assume you know my address, and we look forward to seeing you tomorrow morning."

Chapter Five

The Victims are Connected

As we hurried out the door, Holmes shouted back to Mr. Shepherd. "By nine o'clock if you can."

"I'll be there."

Upon arriving back at Paddington in the late afternoon, we hurried to the line of cabs, but a policeman intercepted us.

"With me, please, gentlemen," he said. "Inspector Lestrade wants you to come directly to Belgravia."

We followed him as he marched smartly out of the railway station to a waiting police carriage. The driver laid his whip to the haunches of his horse, and we bolted away and raced down Praed Street and through Hyde Park. The driver galloped his horses and rang the warning bell furiously as we tore down the Carriage Drive, causing mothers and nannies pushing prams to scamper out of the way. He did the same on Knightsbridge Road, forcing the traffic to part and let us through. Finally, he stopped in front of a terraced house on Wilton Crescent.

We were not alone. There were two more police carriages parked in front of the house, as well as an elegant private coach that was emblazoned with the tri-color flag and the coat of arms of the

Ambassade de France. A uniformed police constable waiting on the pavement pulled open our carriage door as soon as we stopped and bade us follow him into the house.

One member of the Press had already arrived on the scene and was attempting to ask questions of anyone who would take the time to talk to him. No one did. We worked our way past several well-dressed men and a half-dozen more constables and entered the house. Other than thinking that the interior looked … well … very French, I did not have much time to make note of it before we were led into the parlor.

A younger fellow who had been standing against the wall hopped forward to put two chairs in place in what appeared to be a small circle of serious men. Inspector Lestrade was seated in front of the hearth, and the man beside him was, if I remembered correctly, the head of the Foreign Office, the Honourable Talbott Bayless. The only other man I could identify, having seen his picture in the papers, was His Excellency, General Paul Cambon, the French Ambassador. The man sitting beside him looked terribly French, and the two men next to Mr. Bayless looked equally English.

"Holmes!" said Lestrade as we entered. "Glad you made it. Take a seat. Gentlemen, this is Mr. Sherlock Holmes, the most successful consulting detective in the Empire. Scotland Yard retained his expert services the minute we suspected that a madman was bent on murdering highly placed French men and women who were here in London. He has come from spending the day at Broadmoor, where he was making intensive inquiries into this Gaetano Gorgiano fellow who is the crazed criminal whom we suspect is behind these terrible crimes."

"We know Monsieur Holmes," said Ambassador Cambon. "The work he has done in the past for *La France* has been quite commendable, and we to him have awarded the Order of our *Légion d'honneur* for his service. It is good to see that your English *gendarmerie* has learned from our example and is making use of his talents. *Bien sûr*, we would expect nothing less."

I was more than somewhat surprised to hear Inspector Lestrade speak so highly of Sherlock Holmes. For a minute, I was confused, but then it occurred to me that he wanted to make an impression on the ambassador, letting him know that Scotland Yard was taking the matter of the dead French folk extremely seriously and, pulling out all the stops, had even assigned Sherlock Holmes to the case. I gave a sideways glance to Holmes, and he responded with a hint of a wink.

"Now then, Mr. Holmes," said Lestrade, "tell us what you can about this madman. What has he got against our friends and allies from *la République?*"

Holmes, following established protocol, first addressed His Excellency the Ambassador, and then named and nodded toward the entire ensemble of the men who were seated, in descending order of rank. He knew who every one of them was, which was somewhat of a surprise to several of them who, no doubt, had striven diligently to retain their anonymity.

"Yes, Inspector," he said, "we did indeed pay a visit today to the Criminal Lunatic Asylum in Broadmoor. It was quite illuminating. Before imparting what I learned today, may I be so bold as to ask the title and role of the French diplomat whose body, I assume, is resting somewhere in this fine house? Having that data to hand will help me refine my report to you."

I caught a quick glare from Lestrade, but he answered in an unusually courteous manner.

"His name is Colonel Aleron Lamothe, and his position was the Second Secretary for Trade and Commerce. Is that correct, Your Excellency?"

"*Mais oui.*"

"Is that not the office," asked Holmes, all-innocence, "that usually is occupied by the man in charge of all the spies roaming through a country? I know it is for our man in Paris."

The look on Lestrade's face said that he would have happily wrung Holmes's neck, but he kept control of himself and answered calmly.

"I would not know, Mr. Holmes. Why don't you ask your big brother? Now, what can you tell us about this Gorgiano fellow?"

"This Colonel Lamothe," said Holmes, "would I be correct in guessing that his body was dismembered. Were his right hand and left foot removed and placed beside his head?"

"They were," said Lestrade. "The same as was done to Mr. Danton Routhier in the hotel."

"And," said Holmes, "to the captain of the French merchant ship, and to the cheese seller."

"They were all," said Lestrade, "tortured in the same way before being shot in the back of the head."

"Was there a woman killed here as well? And, if so, was she shot and tossed over the balcony?"

"No. His wife is in Paris."

"And his mistress?"

"Was not here at the time. It was she who discovered the body. Now, are you going to tell us what you know, Holmes? His Excellency does not have time to waste."

"Most certainly. The first piece of significant data was discovered before we departed for Broadmoor. It is that the victims have not been selected at random. They are all connected to each other."

"*Vraiment?*" said the ambassador. "How?"

"Your merchant seaman, Captain Darcell Guyse, previously served in the French Navy, did he not? Can Monsieur Dupont, your *ministre plénipotentiaire*, confirm that?" Holmes asked, looking at the French fellow sitting beside the ambassador.

"*Oui, c'est vrai.*"

"Monsieur Routhier was the owner and General Manager, or whatever you call it in French, of the *Manufacture d'Armes de Saint-Étienne*. Was he not? The cheese exporter, Monsieur Fortunio Comtois, only uses Camembert as a cover. He is, in truth, a spy and has served in several places where France has a military or political interest. And now this fellow, Colonel Lamothe, also is directly connected to French army and the *Ministère de la guerre*. Am I correct, Monsieur Dupont ?"

"You are. *Continuez.*"

"It appears that Mr. Gorgiano has selected his victims amongst those French citizens who have a direct connection to your military activities."

"*Mais, oui,* Monsieur Holmes," said the ambassador. "But, of course. However, almost all men of France, those who are *sérieux,* have served as officers in *les grandes armées de France*. It is the most honorable profession in my country. I *moi-même* have served as has every man in this room. Your ratiocination does not help us."

"But it will," said Holmes. "As I continue to investigate, with the capable accompaniment of Scotland Yard, I fully expect to find that the circle of those our killer has selected is much smaller. Once that has been established, we should be able to identify his likely next victims and give them adequate warning."

"Do we know *pourquoi* he is doing this?" asked Ambassador Cambon. "These people are all honorable and respected individuals. There is no blemish on their histories. As the *ambassadeur,* I have files on every French man or woman who sets foot in England. We freely admit that some of our *gens du pays* may be scoundrels, but not one of those who has been murdered. *Alors, pourquoi?*"

"The doctor at Broadmoor speculated that there might have been a French man or two in the hospital who offended him. Perhaps something happened in America that turned him against the French. I consider these explanations to be highly improbable as they do not account for the specific connections we have seen amongst his victims. Either he has a different reason altogether, or it is possible that he has been hired by another party to do their bidding. We are investigating all possibilities and will keep you informed of any progress."

"Right," said Inspector Lestrade. "That's what we expect. So, thank you, Mr. Holmes. Please carry on with your good work. We would not want our French friends to think we were failing to make use of every avenue available to us."

Lestrade stood up, making it evident that our meeting with the diplomats had ended, and we subsequently stood and departed from the parlor. Lestrade followed us.

"Now look here, Holmes," he said once we were out in the vestibule and out of earshot. "I don't care what you do. Just keep me informed on where you go and who you meet with. Right? And if you have to bend a few rules, just make sure I don't hear about *that*. But you have to find this madman and do it on the double. The potentates in Whitehall and Westminster have my arse in a wringer over this. It seems that England and France have entered some talks to have us become formal allies, and having their chaps turn up dead *sans* hand and foot is not seen as a friendly action between friends. So, get to work."

"I shall do so, my dear Inspector. Has the scene of the murder been left undisturbed?"

"It's upstairs. Have at it."

Chapter Six

The Capitoline Wolf and SPQR

We made our way up the stairs to one of the bedrooms. Two uniformed constables were standing guard at the door and, upon entering, I noticed two more men in business suits, sitting in chairs against the far wall of the room.

In the middle of the room lay the victim. He was lying face down in a pool of dried, darkened blood. The back of his head, where he had been shot, was matted with blood. His arms were stretched out above his head and bound with sash cord. His legs were likewise tied together. The horrifying aspect of what we observed was the severed right hand that had been removed and placed beside his face and the severed left foot that lay on his gluteus maximus.

Holmes and I both dropped to our knees to inspect the corpse, and he immediately turned to me.

"Anything strike you as peculiar, Doctor?"

"Two things. The hand and foot have been severed precisely at the joints. The tendons and muscles that linked them to the adjoining bones have been quite neatly severed. Once they had been cut, he could have pried the appendages apart with a screwdriver. Whoever did this has done it before."

"Excellent. Anything else?"

"There is surprisingly little blood from the severed hand and foot. This man was dead for at least several minutes, with his heart stopped, before the amputations took place."

"It appears so," said Holmes. "And that means that he was not tortured. He was executed by the bullet to his head, and then the hand and foot were cut off. I noted the same for Monsieur Routhier. These actions make no sense."

One of the men seated against the wall spoke up.

"Glad we agree, Mr. Holmes."

The chap who said that had a distinctly American accent. I turned and looked at him and observed the slender shape and shaved head of a fellow who bore the look of a military or police officer.

"We have not met, Mr. Holmes, but I have heard about you from my colleague, Paul Leverton. Permit me to introduce myself. The name is Iwan; Michael Iwan."

Holmes was up on his feet and staring at the American.

"And are you a Pinkerton as well?" asked Holmes.

"That I am."

"And just what is it, Mister Iwan, that brings you to this place at this time?"

"Once again, Mr. Holmes, you and Pinkerton's are after the same man. I am trying to track down Gaetano Gorgiano. It appears that you are too."

"I am acting," said Holmes, "on behalf of Scotland Yard. Under whose aegis might you be working?"

"For the *Ancienne Mutuelle de L'assurance* of Paris. They have some scores to settle with Gorgiano, and when they read about his escape, they hired a Pinkerton hawkshaw to make sure he does not murder any more of their esteemed citizens."

"But you're not French, you're an American."

"I was in Paris on another matter, and when the French want to, shall we say, circumvent the official police and government channels, they hire Americans."

"Yes, how very French. And did you follow Gorgiano to this house?"

"I did, but going by the dead man on the floor, I did not arrive in time. I had also run him to ground at the Hyde Park Hotel a few days ago. Again, we were both too late. I assume that you had your Irregulars on his tail."

"I did, but how did you find him?"

"Yankee dollars go a long way, Mr. Holmes, when you need help from some poor immigrants living in Clerkenwell. They tipped me off. Just like your Irregulars keep you informed, they do the same for me. We both almost had Gorgiano by the heels at the hotel, and he still was able to slip in, kill the Frenchman and his wife, and slip out again. If he's a lunatic, he is a surprisingly clever one. Or do you have another explanation, Mr. Holmes? Or can you tell me, Doctor Watson?"

"Just because a man is insane," I said, "it does not mean he has not got a good brain."

"And furthermore," said Holmes, "it may well be that he is not insane at all. And, by any chance, did you happen to find anything that the killer might have left behind? A token of his accomplishment, perhaps?"

Iwan smiled and slipped his hand into his pocket.

"Since you're asking, sir, yes. I found this. The fellows from Scotland Yard ignored it, but I thought it might be significant. And I would be guessing by your asking, that you might have found something similar."

He opened his hand, and, in his palm, I saw a small medallion that bore the symbol of the Capitoline Wolf and the letters S P Q R.

Holmes retrieved two identical medallions from his pocket.

"He is leaving his calling card behind," said Holmes. "These were found in the mouths of the Routhiers. It is his way of taunting the police, the French diplomats, and the two of us. Similar medallions were left behind with the two previous victims. He is brashly telling us that he is Italian."

"He is not only Italian, Mr. Holmes. He is from Naples, and his family is one of the leading clans of the *Camorra*. In your account, Dr. Watson, the investigation three years ago, you referred to them as the Red Circle. Mrs. Lucca said they were part of the *Carbonari,* but she was mistaken. The Carbonari engaged in violence and crime to further their political goals. The *Camorra* only pursue the enormous wealth that comes from controlling extortion, illegal contraband, prostitution, and gambling."

"Are they active in America?" I asked.

"Very," said Iwan. "And we believe that Gaetano Gorgiano was sent to London to establish a cell of the clan here."

"Has he succeeded?"

"Yes."

Chapter Seven

What the Archives Revealed

Mr. Michael Iwan joined Holmes and me for a pint at a tiny pub, the Nag's Head, around the corner from the house occupied by the now-former Second Secretary of the French Embassy. The food and ale were acceptable, and the walls singularly inundated with paraphernalia from across the Empire. The barmaid glared at us when we entered and made it very clear that we were not allowed to loiter at a table for longer than it took to consume our pints.

"Got to hand it to you English," said Iwan. "You sure know how to make a tourist feel welcome."

"If you can assist we English in stopping an Italian from killing the French," said Holmes, "you shall have earned a warm and grateful welcome."

"And until then?" asked Iwan.

"You can learn to enjoy a warm beer and not complain. Now then, what more can you tell us about this Gorgiano fellow? What do you make of his leaving the Italian medallion behind? Do you have any insights into where he might strike next?"

"Like I heard you say to the ambassador, he's after some men who are connected to the military and their war machine. From what little I know about the victims, these men were not just weekend warriors, strutting around in their pillbox hats and singing the Marseillaise. These chaps fought in Senegal, Indochina, Algeria, the Caribbean, China, Madagascar, and all over Africa. Their fathers and grandfathers were military men as well and fought in Japan and Mexico and helped put down the Commune. General Cambon served in Somaliland and claims that Lafayette was his great-great-uncle."

"Not surprising. The French are always at war with someone somewhere. Any direct connection to the Dreyfus Affair?"

"Nah. Like all of France a decade ago, they were divided, but that is more or less settled now. Nobody talks about it in Paris any longer."

"Did they or their forefathers fight against Italy?" asked Holmes.

"A long time ago. But during the past few years, the French and the Italians are kissing and making up. Seems they are both more worried about Germany, and so they better get along with each other."

"Then we are back to some Frenchman having tweaked Gorgiano's nose either in Brooklyn or Broadmoor. But that hypothesis is at odds with his leaving behind a token of Italian pride and nationalism. And why the hand and foot?"

"For sure, I agree, Mr. Holmes. So, I guess that means we both have to keep looking. I'll let you know if I find anything."

"And I will do the same."

When I descended from my bedroom the following morning, Holmes was already present and pacing back and forth the length of the room. His partially eaten breakfast sat on the table beside a half-empty cup of coffee.

"How did he do it, Watson? How did he do it?"

"And a good morning to you as well, Holmes. Are you asking how this Gorgiano fellow managed to slip in and murder someone and not be seen by your sentries?"

"Exactly. I have sent my entire force of Irregulars to work, along with their siblings, legitimate or otherwise, their cousins and even their mothers. They were all on the watch for this crazed Italian from New York. He's a big fellow with black hair and a rubicund complexion and cannot be missed a block away. Iwan has recruited paid agents, and they were on the lookout for him. Yet he entered both the hotel and now the house and committed murder and escaped unseen."

"You are, I assume, discounting any possibility of the supernatural?"

"Watson ... please."

"Right. Well then, maybe there will be something in his record that helps. That chap from Broadmoor should be here shortly."

Whilst I devoured my breakfast, I perused the newspapers that Holmes had left scattered over the table. The accounts of the murders were on the front page, complete with the gory details of the amputations.

On the third page of the *Evening Star* was another in the series of articles trumpeting exclusive revelations from behind the walls. This one claimed that some of the nurses were 'making an extra shilling or two on the side' but did not explain how they were doing it. I tossed it aside and picked up *The Times*.

Holmes continued to alternate between pacing and sitting in his armchair, his legs pulled up underneath his body and his eyes closed. Mrs. Hudson appeared and took away his half-eaten breakfast and scowled at him but, as his eyes were closed, he took no notice. I had just finished my morning cup of coffee when the bell rang, and Mrs. Hudson descended to open the door for our visitor.

"Watson," said Holmes. "Would you mind awfully entertaining this chap for the next several minutes? I do not wish to interrupt my current train of thought."

He departed to his bedroom without waiting for me to answer.

Our guest ascended the stairs and then entered the room. Over his shoulder, Mr. Shepherd carried a large canvas traveling bag that was, I assumed, filled with files on the notorious Red Gorgiano.

I bade him be seated, thanked him for appearing at an hour that must have demanded an early rise, and offered refreshment.

"Mr. Holmes," I said, "shall be with us momentarily. Meanwhile, please enjoy a coffee and do take a few minutes to introduce yourself to me. Our time yesterday was terribly rushed and other than learning your name and that you looked after the Broadmoor archives and records, I know nothing about you. Please tell me more whilst we wait."

"What would you like to know, Doctor? I am John Shepherd, and I look after the records and archives of Broadmoor."

It was the practice of Sherlock Holmes to learn as much as he could about any person or persons who provided data for the cases he investigated. Had he been present, he would have inquired about this fellow directly, bordering on rudely. I chose to be more tactful.

"Forgive me," I said, smiling, "but I suspect that there is much more to your story than that. Pray tell, how did you come to this position of yours and how do you think it might help Mr. Holmes?"

"My home is near Reading, and I chose to be a historian and archivist and studied at Oxford. After working in several places in England, a well-paying position came open at Broadmoor. I applied and was accepted."

"My congratulations."

He chuckled. "Not necessary. It is not easy to recruit people to work at Broadmoor. Many of those who work directly with the patients do not last long. Notices of positions available are often ignored for months before a qualified individual applies. The prospect of being surrounded by criminal lunatics is not one to which many people aspire."

"But you," I said, "have been there for years."

"I work with reports and files, not with deranged criminals. I try to be conscientious and read all the reports on all the patients that come across my desk before I make sure they are filed properly. I know all about our men and women, but I do not have to meet them and talk to them."

"But that burly young chap who led us to your office. He's been there for several years."

"Virgil Bolton? Yes, he's an exception. If you ask him why he has continued to work there, he will tell you that it because he is paid excellent wages, can walk to work, there is no heavy lifting, and he is treated with far greater respect at Broadmoor than his cousins do who work down the road at Sandhurst."

"By the way you have spoken, I assume you find his reasons superficial and disingenuous."

"In truth, he has lasted because he is big enough to not fear being attacked, and he has an unusual interest in the minds and actions of criminal lunatics."

I would have continued with my questions, but Holmes reappeared and wanted to plunge straight away into the reports and files our visitor brought with him.

Mr. Shepherd then began to pull bundles of files out of his shoulder-bag and lay them in distinct piles on the coffee table.

"I read through all of these last evening, sir. These are copies of the court transcripts for Gaetano Gorgiano. I found them quite amusing. The other ones are sorted by department within the hospital. Each has to keep copious notes and submit them to me at the end of each week. Some of the notes from the dietician and the gardener are general and apply to all the patients. The reports, however, of the academic school, and the trade school, and the medical staff are specific to the individual patients. We also have notes from the members of the clergy who conduct religious services and rites on the premises."

"Are they not," I asked, "protected under priest-penitent privilege?"

"Only to a limited extent. If a criminal lunatic confesses to his priest that he is about to break into the women's residence and violate and stab every woman he sees, we assume that the Almighty, as well as the nearest bishop, would want the priest to let someone know. Neither the priests nor the doctors who are sent to us last very long. Most request a transfer within six months."

"Why is that?" I asked.

"From what they have told me, it seems that neither seminary nor years in a parish prepared them for the terrifying experience of confronting evil personified."

"You said," said Holmes, "you found the court documents amusing. Why?"

"You might want to read them yourself, Mr. Holmes. I read through the account of his trial. The Crown produced a dozen witnesses who testified that Mr. Gorgiano was entirely sane."

"Did not his barrister win over the jury by referring to the kitten, puppy and pony?"

"He did indeed. He not only spoke about them, he brought a kitten and a puppy into the courtroom and began to strangle them in front of the jury. The poor things writhed and yelped and screeched so pitifully that no decent Englishman could help but conclude that anyone who would do such horrible things must be a criminal lunatic."

"And the files after his arrival at Broadmoor? Were they also amusing?"

"Not amusing, no. But most were interesting and one was very curious."

"Explain, please."

"The first week Gorgiano was kept in the hospital, he attended Mass and went to confession. The priest noted that he asked him straight out if he wished to confess that he and his barrister misled the jury into believing that he was insane."

"That would seem rather confrontational for a priest."

"He was from Scotland. They're like that."

"And did he record the reply?"

"He did. He wrote that Gaetano Gorgiano asked if it was a sin to present the best possible case in a courtroom because if it were, every barrister in the nation would be destined for the Inferno."

"An astute insight. Anything else from the priest?"

"Nothing. Gorgiano came to Mass every week and to confession and never admitted to anything criminal, and so nothing else material was noted."

"Very well, then. The remainder of the files. What was interesting about them?"

"All the reports from his first two years in Broadmoor state that he was a model patient. He was cooperative, never engaged in violence, and pursued both his academic classes and skilled trades most diligently. In addition to his trade as a mason, he became quite proficient in carpentry and mechanics. He refrained from altercations, was never tardy, and never used foul language."

"That seems highly unusual for any man in such a situation."

"Not unless he is trying to prove that he has recovered from his temporary spell of madness. He was judged *not criminally responsible,* and therefore could not be sentenced to be hanged. If he demonstrates that he has fully recovered, he becomes eligible for release back into the general population. That, indeed, is what happens with most of our patients. Their stories are too dull to make it into the newspapers, and no one expects that a monster who murdered an entire family and its pets would ever be let loose to walk the streets of London. He had, however, a faint hope and was determined to capitalize on it."

"What happened?" demanded Holmes. "Why did he not continue on that course? Did his mind snap? What do the reports say about him?"

"You spoke, I believe, sir, to Dr. Lucheni and his sister?"

"We did."

"Did he not explain what he discovered?"

"Briefly. Pray elaborate."

"It is all in his reports. He used the new techniques developed by Dr. Freud in Vienna and Dr. Charcot in Paris to expose the true thoughts and plans of Gorgiano. Using hypnosis and long conversations, he evoked the plotting of many more torturous murders, and he advised that the patient not be considered for release in the near future and possibly never."

"He appears to have diagnosed the fellow correctly."

"Yes, it appears so."

"Any references to his plans to murder members of the French establishment?"

"They were explicit. He even gave a list of names. Those who are already dead were on it."

I gasped. "Merciful heavens! Then we have to get to those people and warn them."

"I assumed you would wish to do that," said Mr. Shepherd. "I made a copy of all the names noted in the report. I trust you will find it useful."

"Extremely so," said Holmes. "I must act straight away on what you have revealed to me. Is there any possibility that I could prevail upon you to leave these files with me until tomorrow?"

"It is against all of the hospital's rules for us to do so," said Mr. Shepherd, "but it would not be the first time I have broken them. I can leave them with you until tomorrow evening."

Holmes was on his feet and thanked Mr. Shepherd profusely. He did not exactly shoo him out of the house, but he was obviously beyond anxious to act on the data he had been given.

"Come, Watson," he said as soon as our visitors had departed. "We need to get to Lestrade immediately.".

Chapter Eight

The Schoolgirl

We hurried down the stairs and out on to the pavement of Baker Street. I was about to step into the street to hail a cab when Holmes put his hand on my arm.

"Watson, that man, across the street. Look at him."

"Which man?"

"The big one. He's walking away from us now."

I looked and noticed a large fellow who was marching swiftly up Baker Street. Other than his size and his workingman's clothing, I could see nothing unusual about him.

"What about him?" I asked.

"I only saw his face for a second, and he turned away as soon as he perceived that I was looking at him. But he looked remarkably like the guard who escorted us through Broadmoor."

"Shall we try to catch up with him?"

"We can't. We don't have time. I have to get to Lestrade and give him these names straight away so he can protect them. Any delay and another one of them could end up dead and dismembered."

We climbed into a cab, and Holmes shouted to the driver to get us to Scotland Yard and hurry.

"Good work, Holmes," said Inspector Lestrade as he looked over the list of names we had rushed over to him. "Are you sure these are the ones Gorgiano has targeted?"

"Of course not," said Holmes. "All his victims to date are on that list, but there is no certainty that he will attempt to murder the others. However, they are the ones with the highest probability at the moment. I suggest you move with alacrity to provide them with protection around the clock."

"First, we have to find out where they all live and work."

"The Embassy can help us with that," said Lestrade. "They keep track of all their countrymen who cross the Channel and set foot in England."

"Shall we pay a visit to Whitehall?" asked Holmes. "I believe that protocol demands that we arrange such a meeting thorough the officials in our Foreign office."

"Protocol be damned. The Second Coming would be here and gone before those twits get around to doing anything. We're leaving now. Monsieur le Général won't object to our barging in on him if it means saving the hands and feet of his *compatriotes* in England— to say nothing about their heads and brains."

Lestrade stormed out of Scotland Yard, and we followed him and two uniformed constables into a police carriage. The same brace of gleaming black horses sprang out of Scotland Yard and broke into a gallop as soon as we reached The Mall. I feared that we might tip over as we careened around Buckingham Palace, but the driver, who must have raced police carriages many times before, keep us upright and, with the warning bell clanging, we moved at bone-jarring speed up Constitution Hill and into Knightsbridge.

Having forced pedestrians to jump out of our way as we sped around the Wellington Arch, we braked and stopped at the entrance to the French Embassy.

"Constables," said Lestrade. "You lead the way. Just march on past their door and desk staff and up the stairs. The ambassador's suite is at the far-left end of the hall on the second floor. If you think someone is swearing at you in French, ignore him."

The two men in uniform strode through the front doors. The lobby was festooned with tri-color flags that fluttered and as we rushed past. I heard several fellows shouting at us in French and saying the equivalent of *Hey there, where do you think you're going?* in the indignant and supercilious manner of which only the French are capable. We ignored them.

The constables did not stop until the five of us were in the outer office of the *Ambassadeur de la République de France.*

"Is General Cambon in there?" demanded Lestrade of the chap at the secretary's desk.

"Mais oui, mais—,"

"Merci, very much," said Lestrade, and he continued into the large, elegantly furnished office of the ambassador.

I did not have more than a second or two to observe his office, but I could not help but notice all the signs extolling the glory of the republic. There were at least three busts of Napoleon, a framed portrait of Monsieur Émile François Loubet, the President of France, four vases holding massive displays of *fleurs de lys,* and two original paintings by Millet.

"Sorry to barge in on you, General," said Lestrade. "But we need your help if we are going to stop having your *citoyens* getting murdered."

General Cambon stood and gestured us to the chairs in front of his desk.

"Please, gentlemen, say what you have to say. *Parlez, s'il vous plait."*

"Your Excellency," said Lestrade, and then, perhaps as an afterthought and not wanting to violate protocol any further, he gave a shallow bow. "Scotland Yard has been working diligently to stop the murders of French citizens. Our man here, Mr. Sherlock Holmes, has been carrying out a thorough investigation and has produced a list of the French men and women who we believe are the most likely targets of this Gorgiano fellow. When dealing with a madman, no one can ever be sure of what he will do next, but these names are probable, and we need to have these people protected *immédiatement.*"

He handed the list to the ambassador, who in turn nodded to his secretary. They conversed briefly in French, and then the secretary rushed out of the office, list in hand.

"You shall have the addresses of the residences and the places of business of all the names within twenty minutes. I thank you for your diligence."

"You are quite welcome, sir," said Lestrade. "We want our allies to know that we here in England take their concerns very seriously."

"*Merveilleux.* But I have a question for Monsieur Holmes."

"And what is that?" said Holmes.

"Where did this list come from?"

"From officials of the Broadmoor Hospital whom we interviewed."

"*Eh bien.* Yesterday, when you came to the house of Colonel Aleron Lamothe, you had just come from Broadmoor, had you not?"

"We had."

"Why did you not show me this list then?"

"We had not received it until this morning."

"*Bien sur,* so you are telling me that your informants at Broadmoor discovered this list overnight and sent it to you this morning. *Est-ce correct?*"

"No, Your Excellency. We received data regarding Gaetano Gorgiano from two different sources."

"Ah, *oui*. So, you are telling me that one of your sources knew about these names and one did not. *Est-ce correct?*"

Holmes paused before answering. "No, Your Excellency. It would be more accurate to say that both knew, but that one did not disclose it to us, whereas the other one did."

"Does that strike you as odd, Monsieur Holmes?"

"It does ... and I thank you for bringing it to my attention. I will investigate forthwith."

"*Très bien*. On the battlefield, a general must be able to trust his sources of intelligence *absolument*. For a detective, *c'est la même chose, n'est-ce pas?*"

Although the ambassador no longer had the list of names in his hand, he clearly knew who many of them were and chatted on about them, providing us with valuable insights concerning the vulnerability to an attack. I scribbled notes furiously as he spoke.

Twenty minutes passed, and his secretary rushed back into the room bearing a file and handed it to his superior. General Cambon looked it over and gave it to Holmes. He quickly glanced through the pages and looked up at the ambassador.

"This is exceptionally useful, sir," said Holmes. "I am sure that Scotland Yard will have competent men dispatched to the addresses you have given and will carefully guard all the people on the list. However, there is one name for which you have not given us any data."

"*Mais oui?* And which one was that?"

"The ninth name on the list, a Monsieur Alain Dumont Joseph. Do your staff not know this man?"

"They do know him. He is being protected by the Pinkerton man. You will not require any additional constables for him."

"Sir?"

"These are the middle names of a man you already know. I am Paul Alain Dumont Joseph Cambon. You know where I live and where I work."

Holmes and the ambassador looked directly at each other for several seconds. Holmes spoke quietly.

"Our assassin appears to know you quite well, sir."

"He does indeed. *S'il vous plaît,* do not let me detain you any longer. You and Scotland Yard have important work to do."

As soon as we were out of the ambassador's office, I queried Holmes.

"Why didn't Doctor Lucheni tell us about the list of names? He must have written them in the report that Mr. Shepherd brought to us."

"I don't know," said Holmes. "But I am determined to find out. Can you come with me immediately back to Broadmoor?"

Lestrade, Holmes and I quickly exited the French Embassy, followed by the two policemen, and returned to the waiting police carriage. We did not get in. Standing in front of the carriage door was Inspector Gregson, the Scotland Yard officer with whom we had worked on our first encounter with the Gorgiano family.

The look on his face told a story.

"I was about to come and interrupt your meeting," he said.

"What happened?" demanded Lestrade.

"He struck again."

Lestrade looked as if his chest had fallen into his stomach. "Where? No, just take us there."

Once inside the carriage, Inspector Lestrade asked his fellow inspector for whatever preliminary information he had.

"Tobias, can you tell me his name? The victim?"

"It's not a him. It's a her. No sign of any male."

"A name?"

"Celestine Emard. She was a student at the Queen's Gate school."

"Good Lord," said Lestrade. "How old was she?"

"Sixteen. Some of the younger girls at the school came upon her body this morning in the corner of the schoolyard."

"What happened?"

"I only have preliminary data, but some monster did horrendous acts to her body, cut off her hand and foot, and then shot her. There was blood all over the place, so he must have killed her where she was found. Must have happened late last night."

"Have her parents been notified?"

"They're in France. The headmistress told me that she's boarding here with a family in South Kensington. She was sent here to learn English."

"The name of the family she was living with?"

Gregson consulted his notebook. "Breckon-Llewellyn."

"They're Welsh?" said Holmes.

"Right they are, Mr. Holmes. I spoke to them just before leaving to try and find you and Inspector Lestrade. They said the girl was somewhat on the free-spirited side and would often stay out quite late at night. Being as she was French, they did not object, seeing as that's what they thought all French parents let their children do. Even when she did not come down for breakfast, they were not overly worried as she has stayed out all night several times since coming to London. Sowing her wild oats, as they say."

"What this means," said Holmes, "is that our killer has broadened his list of victims beyond the French upper-classes."

"What is also means," said Lestrade, "is if he has added school girls to his depraved deeds, then your list of names is close to useless."

The school was only a few blocks from the French Embassy, and we arrived in less than ten minutes.

I could see a phalanx of policemen standing in the corner of the yard, and they appeared to be holding back a surprisingly crowd of curious onlookers. We hastened from the carriage to the site where the girl's body had been found.

There was no body there.

"What did you do with her?!" Inspector Gregson shouted at the constables.

"Sorry, Inspector, sir," replied the most senior-looking of the constables. "But we had to have her sent to the morgue."

"I told you that nothing was to be touched here!"

"Right, you did, Inspector, sir. But first, we had Headmistress Wyatt come out and tell us that she had a hundred of her girls all screaming and crying and two of her teachers in hysterics, and she told us, she did sir, in no uncertain terms that we were to either get the girl's body taken away or she would come out with her nurse and do it herself, sir. And it had to be gone before the vermin from Fleet Street—her words, sir, not mine—descended on the scene and began to take pictures of the poor child's body."

"Bloody hell, that's no reason for ruining the investigation of a crime scene!"

"We know that, Inspector, sir, and we argued with her. But then a contingent of the mothers of the girls showed up, and they started giving it to us and didn't a clutch of them go and start to move the body themselves. We could see that what happened here was no different from what's been reported happening to all those other French folks. She even had some Italian coin in her mouth, like the papers said the others had. So, we picked her up and sent her to the morgue. Nothing else has been disturbed, sir."

Gregson muttered several unkind words but shrugged his shoulders and turned to Holmes and Lestrade.

"Right sorry about this. But they have a point. It was just like all those others, so not much is lost."

"I suppose not," said Lestrade.

"Don't be ridiculous," said Holmes. "This is a travesty of police work."

"Now look here, Holmes," said Lestrade. "You—,"

"No. I will not look, Inspector. You know perfectly well that every crime scene is unique, and every one offers unique evidence to the investigator. Good day, gentlemen, and I hope that I never again have to face such utter incompetence."

He turned and stormed off. I was about to hurry after him when I was overtaken by a bout of common sense and I walked over to Headmistress Wyatt. A tall, thin student was standing beside her. Her eyes were reddened from crying and she was looking fixedly at the place where the victim's body had lain. I assumed that she had been a friend.

I asked the headmistress if I might have a word with her and took her aside.

After introducing myself, I said, "Madame Headmistress, the gentleman with me was the famous detective, Mr. Sherlock Holmes. He believes that this girl, Celestine Emard, was selected because she was French. Are there any other girls at Queen's Gate School from France?"

She looked at me, and her face paled. She turned and looked at the girl who had been standing beside her.

"Dear God, yes. We have half-a-dozen. Does Sherlock Holmes believe that they could be murdered like that as well?"

"It is possible. Indeed, it is probable. You must take whatever steps are necessary to make sure they are protected."

"I will," she said, her voice trembling. "You may be sure. I will. Thank you, Doctor."

I left her and ran after Holmes, catching up to him a block along Queen's Gate. His clenched fists and forward tilt of his torso told me that he was still furious. I took him firmly by the arm.

"Come now, my friend. A glass of brandy will settle you down. There's a fine pub just around the corner."

He glared at me but said nothing until we reached the Hereford Arms around the corner on Gloucester Road.

After forcing himself to sip a large snifter of brandy and puff his way through a pipe and a half, he seemed to settle down.

"Come now, Holmes," I said. "You must have some sympathy for the children and mothers who were shocked by the sight of a dead body. You and I are inured to such a horror, but those of tender age and delicate sensibilities are not."

"I assure you that I appreciate the distress caused to them. However, they will recover. On the other hand, one does not recover from being tortured and murdered. Tears and hysteria count for little when they impede an investigation directed toward capturing a man who has already killed seven people."

He was right, of course. However, if my years on the battlefield had taught me anything, it was that a man's anger can derail his judgment, and Holmes was no exception.

"My friend," I said, "as your doctor and your chronicler, I can tell that you are under enormous pressure and you and dealing with overwhelming frustration. You always do much better work when you can force yourself into a state of cool reasoning."

He gave me a hard look, but then his face relaxed into a grim smile. "Yes, Doctor. Your diagnosis and prescription are spot on. And you are quite correct. I have seldom if ever faced an enemy who operates as if he is a ghost, coming and going and killing unseen. Every day that passes without my defeating him is a day in which he is free to commit another murder."

"Let me suggest," I said, "that you invest the next few hours in thought and contemplation and that we postpone Broadmoor until tomorrow morning."

"Yes, Doctor. Broadmoor departure at seven from Paddington."

Chapter Nine

A Horrifying Report

In Mid-November, the sun does not rise until well after seven o'clock. Holmes was already up and gone by the time I appeared in our front room, and I departed alone. It was still dark and chilly as I made my way to Paddington. I arrived with fifteen minutes to spare and expected that I would be waiting on the platform when Holmes arrived. As it was, he was there before me and, as I ascended to the platform, I could see his tall, thin figure in the gloom of the gaslights at the far end. He was smoking a cigarette and pacing, with at least three of the morning's newspapers tucked under his arm.

Once inside our cabin, he shared his papers, and for the first hour, the two of us said nothing to each other as we read the stories of the day. The front pages were filled with accounts of the Siege of Ladysmith in the war in the Cape. The troops in the town were struggling to hold out against a much larger force of the enemy, and all of England was praying that they could do so until a relief regiment arrived to save them.

The *Morning Post* included a side-story added to the one of the siege. Their reporter, a young toff named Winston Churchill, had been taken captive by the Boers, and they had received no word for the past several days as to his safety or even if he were still alive.

The *Evening Star* had accounts of the war on the front two pages, but on the third page was another of their 'Exclusive' stories exposing *The Horrors of Broadmoor*. Their young reporter had established links to secret confidential informants inside the hospital, and he had filed several stories over the past two weeks that excoriated the government and the courts for the light sentences they gave to some of the vilest and most depraved criminals England had ever known. Under the byline of a Mr. Devin Brewster, detailed gruesome accounts of their crimes were printed, and the public was warned that under the current laws and practices of the courts, these men could be set free and returned to an unsuspecting citizenry sometime in the future.

The stories were deliberately misleading. The truly dangerous men in Broadmoor would be kept there for the rest of their lives. Those who were released were deemed by the medical staff and the courts to have been ill in their minds and not criminally responsible for their crimes when they were incarcerated. They would only be released once they had recovered their wits, passed all the necessary tests, and considered safe to return to their families and neighbors.

I might have ignored this latest of the sensationalist stories were it not for one startling feature of it. The article was entirely devoted to Gaetano Gorgiano.

The expected facts about the *Assassino Pazzo,* all briefly repeated in this article, were well known. There were no surprises. What was utterly beyond belief, however, were the claims of many direct personal conversations with him.

"Bravely, I listened as the fearsome Big Red Gorgiano told me about his Italian family in Brooklyn," read one sentence, and it went on to attribute a long quote directly to him. Another sentence claimed, "Having risked my life to acquire his confidence, he told me, in horrifying detail, of how he 'executed' (the exact word he used) the Devonborne parents, children, and the family pets."

Either the reporter was a complete liar and the story entirely a fabrication, or he had somehow managed to penetrate the security of Broadmoor and secure direct access to Gorgiano before he escaped.

I looked up from the newspaper and was about to speak to Holmes when I gasped my breath in alarm.

Holmes had a file open on his lap, but his face had lost all its color. His one hand held his pipe and the other a pencil, but both were visibly trembling.

"Good heavens, Holmes. What is wrong?"

He looked up at me, his face ashen, and handed me the file.

"This is the report from the police morgue of the autopsy done on the girl. As a doctor, perhaps you are better prepared to read it objectively than I am."

I took it from him and, in return, handed him the newspaper I had been reading. He shook his head.

"I've read it," he said, and then he stood up, stepped over to the window of the cabin, and opened it, allowing the cold winds of a November morning to blow on his face.

I opened the police file, and within two minutes, was seething with fury and nausea.

The depraved and degenerate violations of Miss Celestine Emard were beyond the horrors of anything I had seen or even heard of in my many years as a doctor. I could not imagine that any human being would do what had been done to this young woman.

"Merciful heavens. If there is a ninth circle of Hell, this man belongs in it. He has completely given his soul over to the Evil One."

"He has," said Holmes, speaking to the sky and passing countryside he continued to gaze out through the window. "And I have been given the task of finding him and stopping him, and I am no closer to doing so than I was a week ago."

For several minutes neither of us said anything, and then I offered, "Why don't you sit down and tell me about whatever you learned from all those files you read yesterday. I might help get our minds off of what we have just read."

He did not reply and continued to stare out the window. Another full minute passed before he turned around and sat down across from me.

"An excellent suggestion, my friend. I will summarize what I learned, and you shall take notes. It would be good for both of us."

I pulled out my notebook and pencil. "Ready when you are."

Holmes leaned back in his seat and lit his pipe. After several slow drafts, he began.

"The first item of note is that much of the data on Gorgiano before he came to England was supplied by the Pinkerton Agency. It appears that they have been running an investigation on the Camorra in America for several decades now. The Gorgiano family immigrated from Naples when our Gaetano was a schoolboy. He was integrated into their operations to run messages throughout New York City and by age fifteen had graduated to a lookout whilst his older cousins and uncles carried out their crimes."

"Was he," I asked, "forced to observe robberies and murders?"

"Possibly, but not likely very many. The Camorra resort to actual violence only as a last resort. Cooperation from their victims is enforced more by the threat of violence than its use."

"They must make a lot of enemies," I said.

"Not as many as one would expect. Do remember that it is America, and every businessman there knows that if you wish to remain in business, you have to keep the customer satisfied. If you are going to demand a monthly payment for providing protection, then you jolly well better provide it. If you expect to make a profit from the procurement of prostitutes, then the chaps who avail themselves of your services had better go home happy, believing that they have received their money's worth. It is a reliable set of business practices for any industry. Young Gaetano Gorgiano was sent to England, ostensibly to attend his Uncle Giuseppe's funeral but, it now appears, to establish a Camorra cell using the same model as is working so well in New York."

"Well, he certainly was not particularly successful, I'd have to say, if he went mad, murdered a family, got caught, and ended up in Broadmoor."

Holmes went on, alternating between recounting more facts and anecdotes from the files he had read and stopping and puffing on his pipe until we had reached the gates of Broadmoor.

Once again, we were greeted at the gate by Virgil Bolton.

Chapter Ten

Learning More about Big Red

We were escorted from the gate and into the grounds by the burly guard. We had gone about fifty yards when Holmes abruptly ceased walking.

"Stop here, Mr. Bolton," he said.

The young fellow looked surprised.

"What for? Is something wrong?

"Yes. Something is quite wrong. I would like to know what you were doing outside of my home whilst Mr. Shepherd was visiting me. And do not waste my time by denying that you were there. Your hulking mass is impossible to miss."

Bolton was taken aback and clearly nonplussed.

"I'm ... I'm not at liberty to say, Mr. Holmes."

"Then get yourself at liberty in the next ten seconds, or we shall continue our meeting in the office of your Director."

Bolton stared at the ground for several seconds and then raised his head and blew a long puff of air up toward the clouds.

"I provide protection," he said, to the clouds.

"Explain yourself."

"Whenever Mr. Shepherd leaves Broadmoor and travels to London, or anywhere else for that matter, I follow him and make sure that he is kept safe."

"Safe? From What? Why does your archivist need to be kept safe?"

"It's like this, Mr. Holmes. You see, Mr. Shepherd has kept the records and archives of Broadmoor for over twenty years. He's read every report that has been put on file, and everything that happens here must be reported. He knows everything that has happened to everyone."

"Are you saying that he knows too much?"

"Well, yes sir. He does. You see, except for the few men and the rare woman who are incurably mad, almost all of our patients recover their wits and are able to return to their previous lives. But whilst they are here, all of their secrets are revealed and recorded and, well, there are many people out there who would do whatever it takes to make sure their secrets are never revealed. They all know who Mr. John Shepherd is, and should they happen to run into him on the streets of London, they might panic, and there is no telling what they might do. So, I tag along behind him just in case. And that's the truth, Mr. Holmes, sir."

"And is that why you insisted that we meet him when we came here before?"

"Yes, sir. I knew that the doctor had only been here a short while and that if you needed to know anything about Big Red, you needed to chat with Mr. Shepherd. Now, sir, I was told you have another appointment with Dr. Lucheni. His office is this way."

Upon our arrival at the doctor's office, he and his lovely sister again graciously sat us down and served us *ciambelle* and superb coffee, followed by a small, chilled glass of *limincello*. Holmes seemed quite content to chat about Verdi and Stradivarius while doing so and I, having also been a soldier, engaged them in sharing a few memories of our times in battle; the two of them in Africa and me in Afghanistan. As with so many doctors and nurses who served behind the front lines, our memories were etched in pain and had we had time for another round or two of *limincello* we might have formed a fast friendship.

That did not happen. Holmes changed the subject and got to the point of our visit.

"When we met you before, you informed us of Gorgiano's gruesome threats against people he considered to be his enemies."

"*Si*, we did. He is an angry and deranged man, and I fear his enemies are not safe from him."

"Why did you not give us the names of the specific people he threatened?"

"Because those names were nonsense. During our first session with him, he named several people and told us what he would do to them, and we entered those names in our report. But the next week, he named two score more. The week after that, another thirty. It was obvious that he had read and remembered the names of many people in the upper crust of London, and all he did was recite their names to us. By the time he escaped, he had named well over one hundred, including every member of the Royal Family. Then at least six inspectors from Scotland Yard, and a certain famous detective named Sherlock Holmes, who lives at 221B Baker Street. The names meant nothing. We interpreted them as indicators of his unspecified rage and nothing more."

"And you did not consider those names to be worthwhile recording?" said Holmes.

"It is not that they were not worthwhile. It was more a matter of their being a distraction. It was far more important to discover the source of his rage and to treat it than to worry about every one of his imagined enemies. There must have seen something in his subconscious mind that was associated with decapitation and dismemberment, and that became the focus of our treatment sessions with him."

"Yes, that makes sense," said Holmes, "and I thank you. Now then, has there been any other data you remember about your times with him that may be useful to our attempt to find and stop him."

Dr. Lucheni said nothing for a minute, but appeared to be carrying on a conversation with himself in his own mind. Like all Italians, he moved his hands vigorously whilst doing so. Finally, he shook his head.

"*Niente.* Nothing. I can think of nothing more. If I do, I shall inform you."

"Thank you, Doctor," said Holmes, and we turned to depart.

"*Signore,*" his lovely sister called to us. "There is something else."

I turned around to look at her in time to catch a scowl directed to her by her brother. He said something to her in Italian that had conveyed the sense of telling her to be quiet. She ignored him.

"What is it, Miss Lucheni?" asked Holmes as he turned and walked back toward her.

"It is not important," said her brother.

"Yes, it is," she said. "It is about the murder of the schoolgirl. I read about it in the newspaper this morning."

"Yes, miss. What about it?"

"The newspaper did not say very much, but it said that Gorgiano had done terrible things to her body. Did he?"

"Yes, he did. Why?"

"That was not like him. He never said anything about hurting young women. If he has started to do that, it is a new direction for him. Maybe it is not even him. It is very dangerous. You must do everything you can to find him and stop him, or more innocent young women will be violated and murdered. You must. It is very important."

Her voice was trembling as she spoke. Her brother came over to her and put his arm around her shoulders, but she shifted away from his touch.

"Mr. Holmes, if he did those terrible things, it is a new evil that has overtaken him. You must stop him!"

"I shall do my utmost, Miss Michelina," said Holmes. He might have said more, but our names were called out by Virgil Bolton.

He had appeared at the door of the medical services office and seemed anxious for us to depart.

"What is it, Mr. Bolton," asked Holmes.

"There's a constable to see you. The fellow from the Crowthorne Constabulary Office."

"Again? What does he want?"

"Can't say, sir. But he was awful anxious, and I told him I would run and fetch the two of you at once."

Chapter Eleven

When the French Came to Sandhurst

"Good morning, Constable Tenney," said Holmes as we departed from the gate of Broadmoor. "What is it this time? Back to London again?"

"No, sir, not to London. If you could please get in our carriage, I have to deliver you down the road. Orders from Scotland Yard."

"Down the road? Where to?" Holmes asked as we climbed into the police carriage.

"Sandhurst. It's only ten minutes from here."

"Sandhurst?" I sputtered. "Good heavens. What happened there?"

"One of their staff, sir, a general. Seems he got murdered last night. They came to my office straight away, and I phoned Scotland Yard and Inspector Lestrade says that Mr. Sherlock Holmes happens to be up the road at Broadmoor so I was to go and fetch him right away quick and take him to Sandhurst and he says he'll be along as fast as he can and will meet you there."

Holmes and I exchanged bewildered glances. It seemed very strange indeed that Lestrade would pull Holmes off of the Gorgiano case and have him investigate a murder amongst military staff.

The Royal Military Academy at Sandhurst is the British Empire's foremost military training institution. For nearly one hundred years, men have entered its walls and grounds and learned the latest in tactics and strategies of the British Army. The list of graduates was a roll call of our most glorious generals and included members of the Royal Family, dukes, earls, and barons of all sorts, and brilliant commoners who went on to earn glory and renown on battlefields all over the great round globe. The citizens of the Empire rightly expected that men who were trained here would be ready to kill any enemy of the Realm. We did not expect them to kill each other.

A young officer in an army uniform met us on King's Walk and directed the police carriage to one of the staff cottages north of the Upper Lake. The small building was ringed with young Army officers and cadets all standing guard. Constable Tenney led the way to the door of the cottage.

"Constable Garwin Tenney, Crowthorne Constabulary," he announced to the Army lads. "On orders from Scotland Yard. With me are Mr. Sherlock Holmes and Dr. Watson. Authorized by Scotland Yard to assist in the investigation. Please stand aside."

They did as requested, and we walked into the cozy, well-appointed cottage. However, once we were in the central hall, our progress was blocked by a chap with the markings of a major in the Military Police on his uniform.

"No offense, Constable," he said. "But this is a military matter, and our own police will carry out the investigation."

"Major, I was given strict instructions by Scotland Yard—"

"Who have no jurisdiction over a crime committed on property of her Majesty's Armed Forces. We will be looking after this matter. Thank you. Our chaps will escort you back out of the grounds."

We were outnumbered and outranked by a large margin, and all three of us turned to leave. As we were doing so, a lieutenant came running into the cottage and handed a telegram slip to the major. He read it and blanched.

"Just a ... just a minute there, Constable," he said. "Please bring Mr. Sherlock Holmes into the bedroom. He has *carte blanche* to carry out an investigation."

We turned back and walked toward the back of the cottage. As Holmes passed him, the major muttered.

"I don't know who you are, but this order came from Number Ten. Someone upstairs thinks this is bloody awful serious."

"In which case, Major," said Holmes, "kindly join me. Your assistance would be invaluable."

We entered the bedroom, and at least one question was answered immediately. Lying on the floor, clad in his dressing-gown, was the body of a man in his sixties. A pool of dried blood surrounded his head. His right hand and his left foot had been cut off. In the blood immediately in front of his eyes, there was a small medallion bearing the imprint of the Capitoline Wolf and the letters S P Q R.

"Blimey," I gasped. "He's going after British generals now. What next?"

"Perhaps not," said Holmes. He stood and spoke to the major.

"Who is this man?"

"He is General Thierry Rainey."

"A Frenchman?"

"Yes, sir. He and one of our Academy staff had exchanged positions. A new program. Just started. Tied to our becoming closer allies with the French. He was teaching our men about the latest French artillery. They have some fine equipment."

"I assume you have inspected the room and the grounds."

"That we did. Hard to say what happened. Nothing out of place in the cottage. There were some marks in the ground up against the fence where someone might have climbed over, but the grounds are not secured, sir. We're on our home soil, here. No one expected that someone would come in and shoot a visiting general."

"Did no one hear the shot? This man has been dead for at least ten hours. Why was not an alarm sounded?"

"The men had a bit of a football game yesterday afternoon. Ended up around four o'clock what with darkness coming early this time of year. It was the end of a long series of exercises, and they were feeling a little obstreperous and got a bit out of hand. A couple of them got to firing off their pistols, and no one took notice of what must have been another shot. We are a military institution, and it is not uncommon to hear guns being fired. It's part of the training."

"Watson?" said Holmes, looking at me. "Your verdict?"

"One shot to the head. Could have been dead since yesterday afternoon."

"The hand and foot?"

"Severed in precisely the same way as the other two. Not much blood, so it must have taken place after he had been shot."

"Major," said Holmes, "might we have a word with you in the front room?"

"I cannot tell you much," said the major after we have moved away from the body and into the cottage's sitting room. "What can I say? He was...well...French."

"Please explain, Major."

"He was terribly bright. Spoke and read several languages. Made it clear that Napoleon was the greatest military genius of all time. Conveniently forgot that we beat the little Corporal Nappy at Trafalgar and Waterloo. Thought that we English were appallingly uncivilized. Refused to eat breakfast in the mess hall with the other officers on staff. Came to his classes fifteen minutes late. You know...*French.*"

"Any visitors?"

"Well, sir, we don't like telling tales out of school."

"He's dead. He will not object."

"Right. Well, he did manage to have a few ...what should I call them—"

"*Fille de joie?*" said Holmes.

"Right. That sounds better than tart or strumpet. Yes, well, he had one or two of them a week come and visit."

I was shocked. "Is that permitted at Sandhurst?"

"Of course not, Doctor. But, as I said, he was French, and this exchange was ordered by the powers that be in Westminster, and we were told to make him feel welcome. It was more than a bit unusual to have a pretty young woman walking through the grounds and over to his cottage. Our fellows—you know how young officers are— they got to changing his name from General Thierry Rainey to *Generally Very Randy*. We had to hold our noses and ignore him, but we had to hand it to him. He knew his stuff. Knew every detail of every piece of artillery in use today, and a hundred years ago, and what new and better designs were coming next from the arsenals in every country in Europe."

Holmes spent the next hour inspecting the room and the grounds surrounding the cottage. When he was done, we were taken back to the train station by Constable Tenney, and we boarded the train back to Reading and then London.

"Watson," he said, turning to me once we were inside our cabin. "How close was the revolver to his head when he was shot."

"Right up against it. There were powder specks all over his neck and dressing gown."

"Yes, that is what I thought as well. And there was no sign of a struggle."

"Someone must have surprised him. Come up from behind," I said.

"Possibly. But he was in the middle of the room when he was shot. The body had not been moved. The only place someone could have been hiding was behind the door that opened to the lavatory. If he was there, he must then have taken several steps to come close enough to the general to put his gun up against his head. You were trained in the army. What would you do if you heard a sound, even a faint rustle behind you that you were not expecting?"

"Turn around straight away, of course, and see who it was behind me."

"Which he did not do. He stood there whilst his killer came up behind him, put a gun to his head and shot him."

"I cannot imagine him letting Gorgiano just do that to him," I said.

"Nor can I."

Chapter Twelve

The American Reports

It was late afternoon by the time we returned to Baker Street. Mrs. Hudson heard us arrive and caught us before we entered the front room.

"There's a man waiting for you, Mr. Holmes. He's been here over an hour and seems rather anxious. I offered him some hot tea, but he refused and just keeps pacing back and forth."

"Why, thank you for letting me know," said Holmes. "Anything odd about him?"

"Well, he's an American, and that's plenty odd enough for me."

Like so many fine English people, Mrs. Hudson could never understand how it happened that Americans had become so rich and successful when they were so obviously inferior to the English in taste, manners, and breeding. But there they were. To be more to the point, *here* they were...constantly; over-dressed, over-paid, over-sexed, over-confident, and over-exuberant.

We entered the room to find the chap from Pinkerton's pacing back and forth. He stopped and exhaled a sigh of relief when we entered.

"Mr. Iwan," said Holmes. "Please, sir, be seated. Terribly sorry that you have had to wait for us. Pray tell, what is the reason for you visit."

He reached for his half-empty cup of now-cold tea and took a gulp.

"We have to stop this monster, sir, and we have to do so before he can kill any more people, and I am willing to work together with you, and I do not care a fig who gets the credit, but we have to stop him."

"Most willing to cooperate, I assure you, sir. But why the great increase in urgency? When we met in the home of the French diplomat, you were much more at ease. What happened?"

"I paid a visit to the morgue. I saw what he did to the girl. He has... he has...I don't know how to describe it. It is as if he walked off the edge of a precipice and descended into hell. What he did in America was criminal, but it was not out of line for warring members of the Italian families. Victims were shot or strangled or bludgeoned, but they were not tortured. What I saw this afternoon was the work of a Satanic madman."

"Was it? The initial data I received from Scotland Yard said that the same distinctive marks of Gorgiano were present—the severed hand and foot, the Italian medallion in the mouth."

"Yes, yes. They were there all right. But there was so much more. I have seen my fair share of murdered corpses in my day, and I have never seen anything that filled me with such horror. The man has snapped. He is killing French people now almost at random."

I agreed with him. "I read the autopsy report. Reading it was enough to sicken me. Viewing the body must have been terribly upsetting."

"We must not," said Holmes, "allow our feelings of horror and outrage to dictate our actions. We still need to learn more about what our killer is doing. This girl was from a well-to-do French family, was she not?" said Holmes.

"She was. Her mother is a famous opera singer," said Iwan.

"And her father?"

"The bishop of Montpellier."

Had I been sipping a cup of tea, I might had choked on it.

"Did you say her father was a bishop?"

"They're French. Don't ask," said Iwan.

"What connection," asked Holmes, "do they have to the French military, government or armaments industry."

"Nothing, and believe me, pal, I checked it six ways from Sunday. Nothing, *nada,* nil, sweet *rien.* If anything, they're pacifists."

For a moment, the three of us sat in silence, and then Holmes turned to me.

"My dear Doctor, is that possible. Can a man's mind snap like that? Turn from conventional heinous crime to something far more depraved?"

"It can," I said, "and it has happened before. Medical science has no explanation. We can neither predict nor can we stop it."

"Will he do it again?" asked Holmes.

"Most likely, yes. To those whose minds have been taken over by evil, it is like the tiger once it has tasted human blood. It cannot be stopped."

"But we've got to stop him," said Iwan. "We've got to figure out what he's going to do next and get him before he does."

"These men," I said, "are predictable in what they will do, but what is unpredictable is where and when they will do it."

"Perhaps not," said Holmes. "Perhaps this one can be tempted."

"You mean, like, lured into a trap?" said Iwan.

"Precisely."

"How?"

"I do not know. Ask me tomorrow."

Chapter Thirteen

Challenged in the Press

The following morning, I hastened to the breakfast table, eager to hear if Holmes had come up with something. He was sitting sipping on his coffee, and his face had that look of determined smugness that he often assumes when he knows he is on to something worthwhile.

"Yes, Watson, I have," he said as I approached the table.

"Have what?"

"Have come up with a plan. That is what you want to know, is it not? Otherwise, why are you coming down to breakfast fifteen minutes before your customary arrival time?"

"Fine. Very well, what is it?"

"It came to me as I reviewed in my mind our meeting at Sandhurst. You recall how the major told us that General Rainey constantly insulted the English."

"I do, yes. What has that to do with Gorgiano?"

"Did the major appear to be furious, highly offended, distraught with anger over what the Frenchman had said?"

"Not at all. Why should he? The French constantly insult us, but no Englishman takes them seriously."

"Quite correct. But why not?"

"Well, because...because we're English. The rest of the world can call us whatever they want. It does not change the fact that Britannia rules the waves and that the sun never sets on the British Empire. Frankly, we find it rather amusing. The music halls are full of clowns dressed in tams and scarves who are jumping up and down screaming insults at us in French."

He smiled. "So they are. But how do the French react when an Englishman insults them? Or reminds them that their national character consists of eating cheese and surrendering? Or what might happen if an Englishman were to fart during the singing of the Marseillaise?"

"Good heavens. That would be *casus belli*. They would be beside themselves with apoplexy."

"Precisely. Now then, what if we someone were to insult the Italians in a way that was even more degrading?"

"Your throat would be cut in an hour."

"And that is exactly what I want."

"You what? You want Gorgiano to cut your throat?"

"No, only to be so angry with me that he loses himself in rage and comes for me straight away when I insult him...and his mother, and his sister, and his saintly grandfather."

"How are you going to say all that to him?"

"Ah, my friend, the Press are good for something."

Readers of my accounts of the adventures of Sherlock Holmes will recall that a few years back, he made use of *The Pall Mall Gazette* when searching for the owner of a goose. That case turned out to be a relatively pleasant one to solve with no lasting criminal consequences. This case could not have been further removed, and

Holmes was intent on stopping Gaetano Gorgiano before he murdered any more innocent young women or Frenchmen.

The office of the *Pall Mall Gazette,* like so many of London's newspapers, was on Fleet Street, not far from Shoe Lane. Upon entering, Holmes gave his card to the young chap at the front desk and asked to see the editor. The lad's eyebrows popped up when he saw the name on the card, and he hurried off down the hall.

Mr. Douglas Straight soon appeared. Holmes would have preferred to deal with his predecessor thrice removed, Mr. William Stead, who had been fearless in his investigation and exposure of vice and crime and crusades to rid the country of the despicable practice of child prostitution and improve the lives of families living in squalid slums. After a few years of using the newspaper as a megaphone for change, he had stepped on too many toes and was removed from his position.

The paper had returned to its 'written by gentlemen for gentlemen' origins, but the current editor was facing stiff competition from several other daily publications and was always eager for an exclusive story about crime; the more lurid, the better for circulation numbers.

"And just what," he said as he approached us, "does Mr. Sherlock Holmes want with our newspaper today? I see you have been called in by Scotland Yard to help find this killer. Might your presence here have something to do with that? If so, you are welcome."

"It does indeed," said Holmes, "although perhaps not in the way you might have hoped, at least, not yet."

"I CAN'T PRINT *THAT!*" bellowed Mr. Straight after Holmes had presented the article he wanted to have run. "It's utterly profane, scurrilous. That language is filthy."

"The nasty parts," said Holmes, "are all in Italian and, pray tell, how many of your readers would understand a word of it?"

"Enough of them."

"Ah, but of those who do, most of them learned it whilst on their tour of Italy, and we can be certain that whilst there they heard much worse and likely uttered the words themselves."

"Fine, Holmes, but what do I get out of this other than having every vicar in the land cursing me?"

"An exclusive story when I catch the killer, at least one day before the story is released to any other paper."

"Fine, but what if you don't catch him?"

"I will."

The following article appeared in the late afternoon edition of the *Pall Mall Gazette* and in all the later editions through to the following day.

THE

PALL MALL GAZETTE

An Evening Newspaper and Review

Famous Detective Calls Killer a *codardo pezzo di merda* and challenges him to a *uomo a uomo* match.

For the past fortnight, London has been terrorized by the vile murders against our esteemed visitors from England's deeply valued and respected ally, La République de France. Mr. Sherlock Holmes, London's finest consulting detective, believes that Gaetano Gorgiano, recently escaped from Broadmoor, is the villain behind the horrific crimes.

"He may be mad," said Holmes, "but as far as I am concerned, he is nothing more than a *testa di cazzo.* If he is truly mad it is because his mother was a *puttana* and *a suo nonno piaceva scopare i ragazzini.* And whilst his grandfather was busy doing that, his sister was a *lesbica promiscua.*

"My message to this coward is that he can *vaffanculo a chi t'è morto.* Like all those pompous young Italians who think themselves to be stallions, he can thank his mother because q*uella bocchinara di tua madre.* If he has the *coglioni* to come and face me instead of killing little girls, I will meet him anytime, anywhere, and engage him in a manly round of fisticuffs. I will give him the punishment he deserves."

Holmes went on to say that only a pathetic coward shoots young women in the head from behind. But what can you expect these days from an Italian from Brooklyn?

When asked where and when he would like to meet the man known as Big Red Gorgiano, Holmes bravely stated that it was up to the coward to name the place.

Londoners are advised to continue to watch this newspaper for exclusive news on the quest to catch the murderous Red Gorgiano.

"Holmes," I said, tossing the newspaper on the floor that evening. "What you said in this notice is utterly vulgar. These words in Italian are disgusting. I cannot print this in an account I might write of this case. Schoolboys read my stories."

"English schoolboys cannot understand Italian. He does."

Chapter Fourteen

The Response to Holmes's Challenge

I had half-expected that Gaetano Gorgiano, having had his honor so unforgivably insulted, would have made contact with Holmes almost immediately and demanded satisfaction. The evening passed, however, with our hearing nothing from him.

At half-past ten, Holmes rose to retire for the evening. He was about to retreat to his bedroom when he stooped, stood still, and then walked over to the bay window.

"Can you hear that, Watson?"

I stood and joined him and strained my ears to hear the furious clanging of a carriage bell.

"Either the police or the fire brigade is rushing somewhere," I said.

"It is getting closer," said Holmes.

Indeed, it was, and a few seconds later, I could tell that someone was tearing north on Baker Street from Marylebone. The sound of the bell increased in volume and was accompanied by the pounding hooves of a team of horses.

They came to a halt in front of 221B Baker Street, and I hurried down the stairs. In spite of my haste, I was not at our door before there came an urgent pounding from the other side. As soon as I opened the door, Inspector Lestrade bolted past me and ascended the stairs, taking several in each step.

"HOLMES!" he screamed as he entered the front room.

"Ah, my dear Inspector, what, pray tell, brings you on a visit at such an hour?"

"Come with me. NOW!"

Lestrade turned and descended the stairs but, being a reasonable man, only one at a time. Holmes and I looked at each other, grabbed our hats, coats and sticks and followed him.

Once we were inside the police carriage, Holmes asked, "Perhaps some explanation concerning our late-night outing, Inspector?"

"It's about your crude little article in the *Gazette*."

"What of it? I have had no response."

"Oh yes, you have Holmes."

He thrust a note at Holmes, who read it and handed it on to me. It ran:

Mr. Sherlock Holmes. Herewith my reply. Have a pleasant evening.

"Good heavens," I sputtered. "Did he strike again? Has he killed another one?"

"No, Doctor," said Lestrade, "he has not killed another *one*. He's killed *two*. This time he's shot and dismembered two blokes, and neither of them is French. One is from St. Petersburg and the other from Addis Ababa."

"At least," said Holmes, "you will not be facing the ire of the French Ambassador again."

"Is that so, Holmes?" said Lestrade. "So, I suppose you think that the toffs in the Foreign Office are all giddy, seeing as they now have dead diplomats from three countries instead of only one."

The carriage bounced and clanged south through Hyde Park and on into Kensington. The streets were almost empty, and there was no need for such a show, but I assumed that Lestrade was eager to impress on us the urgency of the event.

We stopped in front of an elegant white-washed terraced house on De Vere Gardens, in the neighborhood where one finds numerous embassies, High Commissions, and diplomatic residences. Two more police carriages were parked on the street in front of the house, and a line of large constables stood guard along the pavement. They nodded respectfully to Lestrade as we walked past them, and I heard a couple of them whisper the name of *Sherlock Holmes* to the fellow beside him.

As we approached the door, a man who had been standing nearby called out to us.

"Inspector Lestrade! Mr. Holmes!"

"Iwan?" said Lestrade. "What in the blazes are you doing here? You're working for the French, and there's nothing French going on here."

"I have reason to believe, sir, that the murders may be linked to those of the French."

Lestrade looked at Holmes, who nodded his agreement.

"Right. C'mon in then," said Lestrade.

Once inside the richly furnished house, Holmes asked Lestrade to halt.

"Some data would be useful, Inspector."

"Very well. This is the house where the Russkie lived. He is, or I should say *was,* Nikolay Leontiev, *Count* Nilolay Stepanovich Leontev to give him his due. Held some post in the Russian Embassy. The dark-skinned fellow's name is Tedros Gebrselassie.

He is a cousin of sorts to the Emperor Menelik in Addis Ababa, and he worked in their embassy. Seems that they were friends and got along well, and Mr. Tedros often came over to this house for evening supper and drinks."

"I assume you have interviewed the staff and the neighbors. Anything heard or seen?"

"These diplomats are fearful of spies, so there's only one maid who lives in the house. She's Russian, and she was the one who found them when she came home from church. She says that she set out a cold plate for their supper, a large tray of fresh sectioned tomatoes, and two bottles of vodka. It was their weekly ritual. Then she left them alone for the evening. Nobody heard any shots, but that's not surprising since they were in the interior of the house, and these upper-crust homes have thick concrete walls. When the maid found them, they were both lying on the floor, their heads in a pool of blood, and their hand and foot cut off. She runs out of the house screaming bloody murder."

"May I—" said Holmes before Lestrade cut him off.

"They're both in the library. Have at them."

Chapter Fifteen

We are Stumped

The two bottles of vodka sat on the coffee table, neither of them emptied beyond half. The two victims lay on the floor, pools of blood surrounding their heads. Both of them were minus one hand and one foot, with the appendages resting on top of their bodies. There was one difference from the previous victims.

"You can see," said Lestrade, who had followed us into the room, "that they were both shot in the forehead. The killer was facing them when he fired. That made me think it might have been someone else, seeing as they weren't French and all. But they have the same Italian medal in their mouths. So, let me know what you *deduce,* Mr. Holmes. And, for God's sake, find this madman and get him stopped. Tomorrow, this will be all over the press and will probably make it to some politician's speech in the House."

"I shall do my best, Inspector," said Holmes.

He was clearly distraught. The list of victims of this crazed Italian kept growing. Now, he had expanded his targets beyond the French to include other foreigners and a young girl.

"There is something strange about all this," I said to Holmes as he examined the corpses and the surrounding parts of the room.

"There are many strange things," he said, shaking his head. "which of them had occurred to you?"

"I claim no expertise in the medical study of the deranged mind, but from what I have read, it is highly unusual for those so afflicted to kill so many in quick succession. The normal pattern is for them to be sated after one murder and then to wait a week or a month or more for the impulse to do it again reappeared and became irresistible."

"An interesting piece of data, Doctor. Might I add another one, also attesting to the peculiar nature of this specific murder."

"And what is that?"

"Both of these men were shot in the forehead whilst looking at their killer. If you were the second man and had just watched as your friend was shot in the head, would you likely sit still and wait for him to come over to you and do the same?"

"Of course not. I'd at least try to run for the door, even if it meant being shot in the back. At least I'd have a bit of a chance."

"Precisely."

He was still on his knees when the Pinkerton man, Mr. Iwan, knelt down beside him and looked closely at the stubs of the arms and legs from which the hands and feet had been severed.

"I told you," he said, "that I went to the morgue and examined the body of the young girl."

"You did," said Holmes. "You said you were horrified. What of it?"

"There's something else you got to add to your list of strange."

"You already informed me that the merciless things he did to the girl were unlike the way he murdered the others. Is there something else?"

"Yeah, there is. It wasn't only that he tortured the girl, it was also the way he cut off the hand and the foot. It was different."

Holmes stopped examining the carpet with his glass and, whilst still kneeling, raised his upper body.

"Is that so? Pray, explain."

"These cuts, they were made by someone who had gone to medical school. Like Gorgiano. But on the girl, it looked more like an ax had been taken and the hand and the foot chopped off in one fell swoop."

Holmes stood up, and his eyes were now focused on the Pinkerton man.

"Go on. Is there more?"

"Yeah, there is. All the French people, and now the Russian and the fellow from Addis, they all had those Italian medallions in their mouths."

"So did the girl, did she not? That is what the police said."

"Not exactly. The medallions were stamped with *SPQR* and the image of the Capitoline Wolf. The girl had only a two-lira coin."

Chapter Sixteen

And a Child Shall Lead Them

I returned to 221B in the late afternoon of the following day and was not surprised to find that Holmes was nowhere to be seen. Every time I rolled over in my bed the previous night, I heard him pacing the floor and muttering to himself. He kept that up all night. In the morning, I saw him for two minutes whilst he downed a cup of coffee before hurrying out the door.

At five o'clock, there was a knock on the door, and I scurried down to answer it. A bicycle boy handed me an envelope that was addressed to *Mr. Sherlock Holmes.* The writing was sloppily masculine and, when I held it up to my nose, it smelled distinctly of garlic.

Merciful heavens. Is it from him? From the crazy Italian?

I was tempted to open it but thought the better of it and would wait until Holmes returned.

At half-past five, I heard the door open and then the slow, weary steps of my friend ascending the stairs. He entered the room and dropped his body onto the sofa without bothering to remove his coat.

"He is going to strike again, Watson," he said. "I am sure he is, and I cannot stop him. I fully expect that there will be more dead Frenchmen, or Russians or Africans, or even young French girls by the end of the week."

"Maybe not," I said. "Here. This came a half-hour ago."

He looked at the envelope, tore it open, and read the note inside. As he did, an amazing transformation came over him. The weariness vanished. His eyes brightened, and a familiar thin smile of grim determination flickered across his face.

"Come, Watson. Our adversary has responded to my insult. He says he will meet me at seven in Brewery Square in Clerkenwell. Please fetch your service revolver. Best you bring an electric torch as well."

"Holmes, have you gone mad? You cannot just go into a dark square and meet a man who has already murdered half-a-dozen or more people. The man is insane. There's no telling what he'll do."

He handed me the note. It was handwritten messily and ran:

Mr. Sherlock Holmes. You and I need to talk. If you meet me in Brewery Square at seven o'clock, I will enlighten you concerning this case. I give you my word as an Italian and a son of the Church that I will not harm you tonight.

It was signed by Gaetano Gorgiano.

"Holmes, you can't trust this man."

"He gave his word."

"Right, his word as an Italian. I've known far too many Italians and—"

"And as a son of the Church. His eternal soul is at stake when he does that."

"His eternal soul is damned already. You and I know that."

"True. But he does not. Let us go."

It was seven o'clock in the evening and London was dark. The major thoroughfares were lit by incandescent electric light, but many of the smaller streets still depended on gas lamps. We took a cab across London to Clerkenwell and stopped in front of the massive red-brick Cannon Brewery buildings on St. John Street. An unlit walkway between two of the buildings led us into the open space behind them. It was pitch black, and I turned on my torch and shone it around the square. It was empty. There was no sound except for the winds that always blew through November and what may have been the scurrying of a rat across the cobblestones. We stood in silence and waited.

A quiet voice called out. "Are you Sherlock Holmes?"

The voice sounded like a child's, and a small boy emerged out of the darkness and walked toward us.

"I am Sherlock Holmes."

"Follow me please, sir." He turned and walked toward one of the buildings. I shone my light on it as we approached. We were being led to one of the smaller buildings that had the look, even in the night, of no longer being in use. A wire mesh covered the windows, but even with that protection several of them were broken, and the bricking was in need of repair.

"He told me," said the boy, "to tell you to meet him in there. He's upstairs in the offices." He pointed to the door of the abandoned edifice and, having done so, turned and disappeared into the darkness.

Holmes was about to walk inside, and I grabbed his arm firmly.

"This could be a trap. We're not going to come out of this alive."

"I believe that we shall," he said. "And if we do not try, it is a sure thing that several more people will not be alive within a fortnight. We do not have a choice. You do not need to come with me if you think it unwise."

Under my breath, I muttered, "Blast you, Holmes," and followed him.

Chapter Seventeen

We Drop in on Gorgiano

As soon as we were inside, I swept my torch back and forth. The interior of the building was cavernous. The central portion of it had been used for brewing and was filled with rather ancient-looking pipes and vats. A small staircase at the side of the row of vats led up to a third-floor level in which offices had been built along the side of the open area. In the dim light of the torch, I could see that the doors bore the names of those chaps who must have once been the managers and foremen of this colossal wreck of a place. None of the doors had the look of having been opened for a decade or more.

"Up we go," said Holmes as he began to climb the staircase. "Please keep shining your torch ahead of me."

"Holmes, this place is—"

"Structurally sound. Come along."

Up we went. The place was surprisingly clean, except for the detritus of commerce that littered the edges of the steps and the narrow corridor that we entered upon reaching the third level.

"What now?" I whispered.

"Shine your torch ahead and a little to the left. It looks as if something white has been affixed there."

The beam from the torch illuminated a sheet of white paper that had some writing on it. I approached it and read:

Mr. Sherlock Holmes. This way, please.

Underneath the message, he had drawn an arrow pointing to the left. Holmes started walking in that direction. I followed.

"Mr. Gorgiano!" Holmes called out. "We come in good faith and have taken your word as a son of the Church. There are no police officers with us, and we are unarmed."

I felt for my revolver in my pocket. It was not the first time I had known Holmes to lie when being truthful would have been even more foolish than being here in the first place.

The corridor led us along the perimeter of the building until it turned and crossed a catwalk to what appeared to be an open viewing area. In the dim, dark past, a manager must have stood here and gazed out over the operations and watched as his men turned valves, checked temperatures and loaded in water, yeast, malted barley and hops.

There was no way out of the viewing area. We had reached a dead end.

"Holmes, I have a feeling we're not in a safe place anymore."

"At ease, my friend. If he does not come to meet us within the next minute, we shall——"

There was a loud metallic clink, and suddenly I felt the floor I was standing on give way. We had been led to stand on top of a trapdoor. It opened and I was falling down. I screamed. Holmes screamed. It was three stories to the floor of the building. Instinctively, I twisted my body and tried to grasp the edge of the floor. Too late. I kept falling. My military training asserted itself, and I threw my hands behind my head and clasped them together to protect my skull. I was going to break a few bones when I landed but might avoid having my head crushed and killing myself.

I braced myself for what I was sure would be the hard, unforgiving concrete below. My back hit first, and I expected that a few vertebrae would shatter.

That did not happen. I felt myself being absorbed by a soft surface that gave way as I entered it. I had landed in a pile of straw and rolled around and staggered awkwardly to my feet.

"Holmes!"

"I am all right."

I had dropped my torch, but it had remained turned on, and I stumbled through the straw to grab it.

We were inside a large brass vat, at least fifteen feet below the lip. The sides were now oxidized but still as smooth as silk, affording no hope of a handhold or any means of climbing out.

"He's trapped us," I cried out.

"He has indeed," said Holmes, "but he took care not to kill us. Which means he wants to talk. MISTER GORGIANO!"

A voice in the darkness answered from the top of the vat.

"Hey there, Mr. Holmes, Doctor Watson. Sure hope you chaps didn't hurt yourselves. Welcome to Clerkenwell."

Chapter Eighteen

You're Going to Need This

"Some son of the Church you are, Mr. Gorgiano," said Holmes into the void. "You nearly killed us after giving your word that you meant us no harm."

"Aw, c'mon there, Mr. Holmes. It took me an hour to get all those bales dumped down there. Did you like the contraption I built for you? Real humdinger, isn't it? Learned all that carpentry in Broadmoor. Never knew it would come in so handy."

"I am sure you did not ask us to meet you so you could show off your peculiar skills."

"Nah, you're right. I wanted to meet with you because of all those insults you made about my family."

"If I offended your honor, you may be sure that I intended to do so."

"My honor? Hey, honor, schmoner. I wanted to find out how you knew all those things about my family. How did you know that my *nonno* was a perverted old so-and-so? We were always having to keep him away from the neighborhood children. And you knew somehow that my sister didn't like men at all, any of them. And my *mamma* ...how did you know what she did to keep food on the table and herself in furs. Tell me. How did you know all that?"

I was about to shout back, *"He didn't. He made all that up,"* but Holmes took another tact.

"And does your lack of honor extent to utterly shameful acts done to young girls. I am quite certain that your *noono* and *nonna* would be humiliated if they heard what you did to her."

"Hey, now that wasn't me. I would never do anything like that. That was disgusting, and whoever did it tried to make it look like it was me, but it wasn't. Not no way and no how."

"Then who was it?" asked Holmes, directing his questions to the disembodied voice in the darkness above us.

"That's for you to figure out, Mr. Hackshaw. But you better get a move on finding him. I know those mad men. There were a few of them in Broadmoor, and they never stop once they start. But I would never do nothing like what they did. I'm not *pazzo*."

"You were convicted of killing an entire family, including the children and the household pets. How do you now claim you were not mad?"

"Hey, that wasn't anything personal. It was business. That Lord Devonborne had our contract for the whole South-west of England. We had a deal with him, and he welched on it. Lied to us. Cheated us. We couldn't let that happen. Once you let anyone do that to you, everyone will. We had to make an example of him. You know, a deterrent. Just like the way they used to let people watch a hanging. Nothing crazy about that."

Occasionally, I would sweep the beam of my torch up through the darkness, trying to catch a glimpse of the man whose prisoners we had become. He must have been sitting back from the edge of the trapdoor, for I could see nothing of him. I turned off my torch to preserve the battery, and the conversation continued in complete darkness.

"What about all those French folks?" asked Holmes. "They did nothing to cheat you? Killing them looks like madness to me. If you give yourself up to the police, you have a good chance at court of again being declared insane and sent back to the hospital instead of the gallows."

"Jeepers there, fella. I can't do that. That's a real bonehead idea. I'd have every Frenchie in the madhouse coming after me. And besides, it wasn't madness to get rid of them. I made a deal, and if you make a deal, you gotta honor your word. There ain't no loopholes in a handshake is what my Uncle Giuseppe used to say. Nope, all I got to do is look after one more of those fellows, the Great Panjandrum Himself, and then my part of the deal is over, and I'm goin' back to the Excited Mistakes of America."

He laughed at his self-appraised wit.

"If that is your intention," said Holmes, "what was the purpose in trapping us?"

"Well, if you must know there, Mr. Hawkshaw, I wanted to meet the famous Sherlock Holmes."

"Fine. You've met me, now kindly provide me with a ladder. I will give you my word that we will not climb out for at least fifteen minutes, and you can escape."

"Nah, ain't gonna do that. It's like, you know, I gotta keep you out of my way until my work is done. You were getting too close for comfort. Somebody will be along within the next two days to get you out of here. You won't die before then. Might get awful uncomfortable, if you know what I mean. But hey, I'm a decent sort of fellow. Here! You're gonna need this."

I heard several loud metallic clangs followed by the thump of something landing on the straw. I turned on my torch to see a large chamber pot.

"Have fun down there. Gotta go now. Nice meeting you."

"Hold on a minute," Holmes shouted back, but to no avail. Our captor was gone.

Over the next hour, we tried shouting for help. Holmes blew countless blasts on his police whistle. The only response was an echo from within the cavernous building, followed by total silence.

I let Holmes step up onto my shoulders, and from there, he attempted to leap up to the edge. He failed and came crashing down on top of me. All I would have to show for that effort would be badly bruised shoulders.

We sat down on the straw and waited.

Chapter Nineteen

Go Get a Ladder

After what seemed an eternity, I flashed my torch on to look at my watch. It was only ten o'clock.

"How long," I asked, "before anyone comes by?"

"Morning at the earliest. These buildings are inspected weekly, and the neighborhood children no doubt find them fun to play in."

"How do you know that they are inspected weekly? I've never heard of that."

"Neither have I, so I made it up. It would not do to have you lose hope."

"Thank you so much for your consideration."

"Anytime, old chap. I will make good use of the time to catch up on sleep."

Within ten minutes, his breathing settled into the regular rhythm of a man asleep. Mine did not.

The next time I looked at my watch, it was approaching midnight. In the undisturbed silence and darkness, I could hear the faint sound of my heart beating.

Then I heard another sound. Someone was in the building. I was about to shout when the thought occurred to me that whoever the visitor was, there was no way to tell if he was friend or foe. In silence, I wriggled my body over to Holmes's and gave him a solid kick.

He twitched and gasped awake.

I whispered. "Ssshh. Holmes, there is someone out there."

He listened, and we could both hear the distinct sound of footsteps ascending the narrow staircase to the level of the offices. Whoever it was, he was now following the instructions and arrow Gorgiano had left for us. Looking up through the hole left open by the trapdoor, I could see the unnatural flashes from the beam of a torch and sensed that he was approaching the hole through which we had fallen.

"SHERLOCK HOLMES!" a voice called out.

"It's the Pinkerton man," Holmes whispered to me, and then he shouted back. A moment later, a beam of light from a torch was shining down on us.

"Good grief, what are you two chaps doing down there?"

"More to the point," said Holmes, "what are you—"

I gave him a hard elbow and interrupted.

"Mr. Iwan," I said, "could you please go and find us a ladder? We can chat about other matters once we are out of here."

"I'll see what I can do. It may take me a while."

It took him an hour, during which time I sat uncomfortably on the straw with my legs crossed.

A ladder that was shorter than I would have preferred by at least six feet appeared in the trapdoor hole and was lowered into the vat.

"See if this works," said Iwan. "It was all I could find in Clerkenwell after midnight. The pub on Goswell Street was still open, and I had to leave a fiver with the publican to guarantee I'd bring it back."

The feet of the ladder descended into the layer of straw, leaving the top of it at least seven feet short of the rim of the vat. I climbed up, but even with my feet on the uppermost rung, my fingers were several inches short of anything I could grab hold of.

"Holmes, you'll have to climb up behind me so I can stand on your shoulders."

Had anyone been watching, the two of us must have looked like circus clowns about to tumble down in comic relief. Nevertheless, with Holmes on the ladder and my feet on his shoulders, I was able to find purchase and pull myself out, with considerable help from Mr. Iwan. Holmes, being significantly taller than me, was able to reach the edge on his own, and the two of us at the top hauled him up.

"Thank you, sir," said Holmes. "Now then, just what brought you to this obscure location at midnight?"

"My spies," he answered. "They told me that a chap matching the description of Gorgiano had been spotted in the neighborhood, and I came here looking for him. I wandered up and down every street and alley and stopped in every pub before noticing this vacant building."

"And a good thing you did," I said. "Shall we help you take the ladder back to the pub? I'm sure that publican would welcome its return."

I confess that my motive in wanting to make a hasty visit to the pub had nothing whatsoever to do with a ladder.

Once that errand had been accomplished, the three of us ordered a very late round of brandy, compared notes, and talked about what to do next.

Chapter Twenty

We Warn the Grand Panjandrum

"Do you believe him?" I asked Holmes, "when he said he did not kill the girl?"

"Hard to say for certain, but I am inclined to do so. We have the evidence that the method of dismemberment was different, as was the item left in the mouth. And no violation was inflicted on Madame Routhier, even though the opportunity to do so was present. So, it is possible he is telling the truth on that one, although with these fellows who end up in Broadmoor, you can never tell if they are telling the truth or lying."

"Well, that would be a bit of a relief. At least we now don't have to worry about him murdering another French girl."

"I beg to differ, my dear Doctor," said Holmes. "What it means is that if there are indeed two murderers, we know only one of them, and the other, we do not know at all. If there is a second, he appears to be mimicking the first with the demented hope of continuing to do unspeakable evil whilst directing the suspicions toward Gorgiano."

"So, what do we do now?" the Pinkerton man asked Holmes.

"If you ask me," I said, although he had not, "I think we should not let on that we are out of the brewery vat. Let Gorgiano think we are still trapped, and we can keep on the lookout for him and take him when we find him. Your Irregulars, Holmes, can be posted all around here, as can your spies, Mr. Iwan."

"A spanking good idea," said Iwan.

Holmes said nothing. He puffed on his pipe in silence for a minute before offering his thoughts.

"Perhaps not, gentlemen. Your suggestion has merit, but we already know where he is going to strike next."

"Where?" I asked. "He could kill anybody anywhere, or so could the second killer. If indeed there is one."

"Gorgiano said something about having only one more job to do, and that was '*the Grand Panjandrum.*' Who might he have meant by that?"

"I have no idea," I said. "The Queen? The Prime Minister?"

"If he sticks to the French," said Mr. Iwan, "then it would have to be the French Ambassador."

"I am inclined to agree, sir," said Holmes. "Therefore, we must warn General Cambon, but in doing so, we must sacrifice any hope of having our escape from the brewery remain a secret."

"Could we not," I said, "tell all those French chaps that they have to keep a secret?"

Both Holmes and the Pinkerton man looked at me as if to ask if I had bidden my brain adieu.

"Oh."

We said goodnight to Mr. Iwan, and Holmes and I found a cab back to Baker Street. It was past two o'clock in the morning when I was about to leave Holmes sitting in his chair and smoking and stagger up to my bedroom.

"Holmes?" I said before leaving him.

"What now, my friend?"

"Are you sure about the French Ambassador? How do the chaps from St. Petersburg and Addis Ababa fit in? They weren't French at all."

"They fit in quite acceptably."

"They do? How?"

"I do not know. But I am sure they do, and they are one more item on my list of puzzles to solve. Do get some sleep, my friend. Good night."

Ten o'clock the following morning found Holmes, Mr. Iwan, Inspector Lestrade and me in a room at the French Embassy in Knightsbridge. It was a Monday and the staff had all arrived and were at work.

"*S'il vous plaît* gentlemen, attend here," said the uniformed official. "His Excellency will be with you *bientôt.*"

From my schooldays, I remembered *bientôt* meaning *soon,* not an hour later, and I grumbled something to that effect.

"At ease, my good Doctor," said Holmes. "You must also remember that they are French."

At a quarter past eleven, the French Ambassador, General Paul Cambon, entered the room along with two of his aides. Mr. Iwan stood and nodded toward him. Lestrade half stood and nodded almost imperceptibly. It was apparent from the glares visited upon Holmes and me by the two aides that we were also expected to jump to our feet and bow or genuflect or some similar gesture of obeisance. I glanced at Holmes, who had not so much as extinguished his cigarette and remained glued to his chair. So did I.

"Monsieur Holmes," said the Ambassador, "this had better be *très important.* I am in the midst of cordial meetings and—"

"If you consider your life important," said Holmes, "and keeping your hand and foot attached to your body, then I suggest you sit down and listen."

The room went silent. Inspector Lestrade covered his mouth and feigned a cough in what I took to be a struggle not to grin.

"Speak," said the Ambassador, but he remained standing.

After a slow puff on his cigarette, Holmes said, "The evidence we have acquired strongly indicates that this crazy Italian killer may have only one murder left to commit and that will be you. Now, if you would like to know more, I suggest, with respect, that you take a seat and listen. We can work together to find a way to capture him before he does."

The Ambassador sat down.

"What is your evidence?"

Holmes recounted our meeting with Gaetano Gorgiano and his assertion that he had one final act to carry out. His Excellency was not familiar with the sobriquet *The Great Panjandrum.* Inspector Lestrade very diplomatically informed him that it was a term borrowed from an English story and meant a person of great power and authority, astutely leaving out any reference to pomposity, pretension and self-importance. General Cambon agreed with us that, under the circumstance, he alone would be the logical person to equate with that title.

"*Alors,* and what is your plan?"

Chapter Twenty-One

I Am a Soldier

"General," said Holmes, "as the Ambassador of France, you are acknowledged to be the one whom all the people of France living in London look to for leadership. Would you agree?"

"But of course."

"As their leader, you are deeply troubled by the horrible sufferings of the victims of the mad killer. Your heart is grieved by all that has happened. Would you agree?"

"If you say so, *continuez*."

"Therefore, it is appropriate that you take time from the illustrious affairs of state to remember those whose lives have been lost. As a devout Catholic man and a friend of the Archbishop of Paris, you have taken it upon yourself to spend a day in prayer for their souls. You are a man of prayer, I assume."

"All generals say prayers, but they are very short, and we do not close our eyes."

"Quite understandable. Tomorrow, you will have to make longer prayers. You will leave the Embassy first thing tomorrow morning and go to the Church of the Immaculate Conception. It is close to here. Are you familiar with it?"

"*Oui, bien sir.* It is in Mayfair and is run by the Jesuits. As far as I am concerned, those Jesuits are *un pertain demerger.*"

"Our English Jesuits are not so inclined, I assure you, and Father Ignatius has agreed to have a comfortable prayer pad available so that you can spend all day before the altar praying for those departed souls. The killer will know about your plan because you will so inform your staff of your intention, and one of them who can be counted on to pass along state secrets to the Press will no doubt do so."

General Cambon stiffened. He rose from his chair and pointed his finger at Holmes.

"How dare you! My men are loyal to me and—"

"Oh, puhleeese, General. There is no such thing as state secrets. Whitehall has spies in your Embassy just as you do in ours. You know perfectly well that if a matter is told to all of your staff, the Press will hear of it before tea time."

His Excellency sat down.

"*Peut-être.* And you believe, do you, Monsieur Holmes, that this killer will take advantage of my being alone at prayer to try to kill me?"

"Precisely."

"It is a clever plan. Let me think about it."

"There is not much time available for review," said Holmes. "However, while you are thinking about it, may I ask another question?"

"*Quoi?*"

"Has there been any encounter in the past few decades when the Italians fought against an alliance of the French, the Russians, and the Abyssinians?"

"*Quoi?* No. The Russians are friends of France and have been for years, but we have never joined them in fighting Italy. And we have never fought with or against the Abyssinians. Why would we?"

"My curiosity. Thank you. Now then, have you finished thinking about my suggested plan? You are a man of action, and neither of us has time to dawdle."

I thought the general was going to burst a blood vessel, but he unclenched his fists and smiled at Holmes."

"There is something about your style, Mr. Holmes, that I like. You move quickly. That is good. And yes, I have thought about it. I like it. Nevertheless, I cannot spend an entire day doing this. Treaties affecting the future of war and peace are being negotiated. I do not have the freedom of spending a whole day waiting for someone to shoot me."

"We thought of that, sir. I have had a wax model of you prepared. All you will have to do is walk from here—under guard, of course—to the church. You will walk in, but we shall place a model of you in front of the altar, and you will slip out the back from the Lady chapel, return in secret to the Embassy and get back to work. Inspector Lestrade will have his men hidden throughout the church, ready to apprehend the killer when he appears. I have carried out a ruse like this before, and it succeeded. I expect it will again."

General Cambon interlaced the fingers of his hands, placed his hands on the desk in front of him and scowled at them. A minute later, he stood up and paced back and forth through the room.

"No, it won't work," he said as he paced.

"I assure you, sir, it has worked for me—"

"*Non! Pas possible.* What worked for you will not work here. It is a good plan. *Oui.* Except that the minute I return to the Embassy, whoever amongst my staff who told the Press my plans will find a way to tell them of my return. The Press will call me a *poseur,* and the killer will be warned away. No, Monsieur Holmes. This is what we need to do. I must go to the church and stay there and be prepared to be a live target for this insane killer."

"Sir, that is very courageous, but it could be dangerous."

"Allow me to remind you, Mr. Holmes. I am a soldier."

Chapter Twenty-Two

The Clue in the Signatures

saw nothing of Holmes for the remainder of the day and returned from my surgery to 221B around tea time. I had purchased a late afternoon newspaper on my way home and opened it to read a short article announcing the intention of the French Ambassador to spend the next day in prayer. I ignored yet another sensationalist exposé about Broadmoor.

That news traveled quickly, I said to myself and tried to relax over a cup of tea and biscuits Mrs. Hudson had kindly prepared.

The bell rang, and our dutiful landlady descended to open the door. She returned a minute bearing a gentleman's coat and hat and was followed by Mr. John Shepherd.

"Sir, what brings you from Broadmoor?"

"Is Sherlock Holmes in?"

"No, not at present."

"When will he return?"

"Quite honestly, Mr. Shepherd, I have no idea. He is working on this Gorgiano case, and he may be out all night. Can I help you? Please, take a seat and have a cup of tea. It's a fresh pot, and the biscuits are excellent ... and, quite frankly, you look a little peaked. Is everything all right?"

"No, Doctor. It is not. I did not sleep at all last night, and I left to come to London as soon as I could get away from my responsibilities at Broadmoor."

"Good heavens. What's wrong?"

He sighed, reached inside his suit jacket, pulled out a file, and laid it on the table.

"I cannot stay, Doctor, I fear I shall have to leave these with you and trust you to pass everything along to Mr. Holmes. It might have something to do with this Gorgiano case he is working on."

"I have been so entrusted many times in the past. Whatever you need to convey to him, I can assure you will be done so in complete confidence."

"I suppose that will have to do, and then yes, I will have a cup of tea. I rather need one."

I poured one for him but could not stop looking at the folded reports.

"Did you wish to explain these to me?" I asked.

"It is possible that what came to my mind when I read them is entirely wrong. But there was something in them that bothered me, and I decided that I better bring it to Sherlock Holmes. Please apologize to him if he sees it as a waste of his time."

"I am sure he will appreciate the effort you have made to assist him. So ... pray tell, what is in the reports?"

"They go back five years now, and they are all reports about one of our most dangerous patients, a fellow by the name of Archibald Castellucci. He killed seven people up in Newcastle and was declared to be a criminal lunatic and sent to Broadmoor."

"I don't remember that name," I said.

"No, it was kept from the Press because of the identities of some of his victims."

"Ah, and were they French by any chance?"

"No, but they were all schoolgirls."

I put down my cup of tea and picked up the reports. The earliest reports were from his trial and gave details of his horrific crimes. Most of the other reports were more recent and seemed to be of a quotidian administrative nature.

"This fellow was a monster," I said. "What he did to those girls is beyond belief. He's just like whoever killed Celestine Emard. The same pattern of violation and torture. Is there some sort of Satanic ritual that more than one man has been part of? Do they belong to a club, a cabal where they exchange their conquest stories and compare methods?"

"One might think that," said Mr. Shepherd. "Now, please observe the other reports."

I did. They were all standard hospital forms for those who were confined to an institution for an extended period of time. Socks, shirts, underwear, shoes and hygiene items were all provided on a regular schedule and had to be signed for, confirming receipt. All hospitals had a similar practice, having found it necessary to keep items from vanishing between the warehouse and the patients' rooms. All the forms I looked at were of items delivered to Mr. Archibald Castellucci and were signed for by him. Nothing appeared out of the ordinary.

"What am I not seeing, sir?" I asked.

"Compare the signatures over the time covered by the reports."

"I can see that they are not exactly alike, but is that unusual for a man who is mentally deranged and confined to a place like Broadmoor?"

"Not at all. But please look at the most recent two forms and compare them to the others."

I did, and then I got up and walked over to the mantle and picked up one of Holmes's magnifying glasses.

"They are still reasonably similar," I said, "except for the recent one having been somewhat more smudged. A different pen perhaps that flowed more ink."

He looked at me and said, "Yes. Please go on. In which direction do the recent smudges point."

"They all go from left to right. He must have been left-handed and..."

I stopped and looked again at the earlier signatures.

"Good heavens. He switched from writing with his right hand to his left. How odd."

"Odd, Doctor? How many people do that when past the age of twenty?"

"It's rare but not impossible. The only other reason is if... Oh my goodness, these were signed by two different men!"

"That was what I thought as well, Doctor. Might Mr. Holmes find this of use in his investigation?"

"Most certainly he would."

"I was hoping so. Now, if you will excuse me, I have to catch the late train to Reading."

He departed, and I sipped cold tea and paced back and forth until Holmes finally appeared at six o'clock.

"Holmes! You must look at these," I said as soon as he entered the room.

"Later, Watson. We have a dinner engagement. Please don your coat and hat. We need to be off."

He turned and walked back down the stairs and out onto Baker Street.

Chapter Twenty-Three

Bottle of Red in an Italian Restaurant

"Holmes!" I said as I clambered up into the cab. "You really must see this."

I thrust the file into his lap.

"My dear Watson, in case you had not noticed, at six o'clock in the evening, it is too dark inside a cab to read. You will have to tell me whatever it is you want me to know."

I told him. It caught his attention. He lit a match to give a few seconds of light.

"Do you have the forms showing the change of hands used for signing?"

I handed them to him, and then I lit a match so he could see for the few seconds before the flame began to scorch my fingers.

"There is something here," he said. "However, we shall have to leave this second killer until we capture the first."

"Are we on our way to catch him now?"

"Heavens, no. We are going to dinner at Goldini's."

"That garish Italian place? What in the world for?"

"I wish to be as prepared as possible for our encounter tomorrow with Gorgiano. The two people who know him best are Dr. and Nurse Lucheni. I invited them to be our guests for dinner. As Italian restaurants are non-existent where they live, I made them an offer they couldn't refuse, and we are taking them to dinner at the most convenient Italian restaurant to Baker Street, garish or not. Goldini's has an extensive menu, and I am sure there will be something on it to their liking. It is good, is it not, to show appreciation to those who assist us?"

Of course, it was, and as I thought about it, I began to fancy a fine plate of veal parmigiana.

I had not been to Goldini's on Gloucester Road in Kensington since Holmes and I ate there prior to our breaking into the house rented by Hugo Oberstein. It had not become any less garish since the time of that adventure. The table cloths were checkered with red and white, each adorned by a candle set in a basketed bottle of Chianti. The waiters all wore a formal suit with full tails but covered by an apron that had been some shade of white in the earlier hours of the afternoon. Occasionally a guest who had not been warned against doing so would ask the troupe of waiters to render a round of the recently popular song, *O Solo Mio*. This they did whilst waving their white linen towels as they sang. The enjoyment of the food was not enhanced by the approximation of music.

Holmes seemed unusually relaxed given the horror of the crimes he was investigating.

"A coffee and curacao?" he asked me. "It will help you to relax and enjoy the dinner and conversation."

"Only if you do."

"As much as I might like, best we not. I hope to encourage our two informants from Broadmoor to speak freely and, as neither of us should despoil the dinner by taking notes, our minds and memories must remain sharp."

"Then best you offer the coffee and curacao to them."

"An excellent suggestion, although, if I recall, they were more disposed to *limcello,* and here they are now."

Dr. Tito Lucheni and his sister, Michelina, had arrived and were approaching our table, smiling warmly. She was leading the way, and he was limping along behind her.

Having slid the Broadmoor under my chair, I stood and greeted them, giving the doctor a friendly clap on his shoulder.

"How's that old Africa wound? Looks like it's bothering you a bit."

"On a November evening, it becomes uncomfortable, *si,* but it is a small price to pay for the promise of a fine dinner in London."

"Ah, Signore Holmes and Dottor Watson," said Miss Michelina, "such a wonderful idea. *Splendida.* It has been so long since we have enjoyed a meal of real Italian food that we did not have to prepare for ourselves. This is very thoughtful of you."

The waiter arrived with a tray bearing four glasses of *prosecco.* Holmes proposed a toast to the growing friendship between the nations of Italy and England, and we toasted the future. When the waiter came to take our order for the *antipasta,* Holmes insisted that our guests order on our behalf. They did this with obvious pleasure.

"And a bottle of wine to start the evening," said Holmes. "I am rather partial to a Taurasi from 1875 or earlier. Would that be suitable for the two of you?"

Nurse Michelina gasped with delight. "Oh, do they have it here? That would be *favoloso.* We used to drink that wine around the family table at *San Januarius.* It has been years since I enjoyed it. It is such a perfect way to bring cheer in cold and dark November."

A bottle arrived at our table, and we toasted each other. When it came time to order the *primo* and *secondo,* Holmes again asked our guests to do the honors. They asked for *Spaghetti alla puttanesca,* to be followed by *Pesce al Forno con Salsa Verde.* Holmes ordered another bottle of wine.

Over supper, Holmes, in a friendly and charming manner, interrogated the two of them concerning Gaetano Gorgiano. Every detail of his life was dissected, from his childhood to the day before he escaped. They responded to the best of their knowledge, noting that they had had only a limited number of sessions with him. They both expressed deep concern over the murder of the young girl and were surprised to hear that her school was only a couple of blocks from the restaurant. Miss Michelina repeated the warning she had given Holmes when we visited them at Broadmoor, stressing again that a dangerous turn in Gorgiano's mind and behavior must have taken place. Holmes did not mention our suspicions that there might be a second killer on the loose.

During the *dolce* course and half-way through the third bottle of wine, Dr. Lucheni posed a few questions of his own.

"Have you made any progress in tracking him down? Is there any possibility of his killing again and then escaping one more time?"

To my surprise, Holmes told them about our encounter in the brewery and then about the plan for entrapping the killer the following day at the church.

"I read in the newspaper," said Dr. Lucheni, "about General Cambon's plan to spend the day in prayer. I was appalled that you would let such knowledge become public as it would be an open invitation to Gorgiano to strike, but now I can see that it makes much more sense. If you and Scotland Yard are lying in wait for him, it is an excellent plan. We shall say prayers ourselves for your success."

"Do you have any advice about how to approach him? What is he likely to do when he sees the police?"

Miss Michelina said something in Italian which, in a Bowdlerized translation, might be rendered that he would kick the contents of their intestine out of them.

"Si," said her brother. "He is a fighter and a very strong one. It may be impossible to take him alive. The police had better be well-armed."

Holmes thanked them for their sage advice, and we returned to chatting about the current leading Italian football team, the splendid athletes from Milano. The evening ended with a final round of *limoncello.*

It had gone ten o'clock when the doctor and his sister departed the restaurant. Miss Michelina required the stabilizing support of her brother's arm to keep her from tottering as they made their way out on to Gloucester Road.

"Well, Holmes," I said as we sat at the table after our guests had gone. "That was a truly excellent meal and thoroughly enjoyable conversation, but did you learn anything new and useful?"

"Perhaps not as much as I had hoped for, but enough to justify the bill."

"I do hope you took note of the warning about how dangerous Gorgiano can be if cornered."

"What? Oh yes, that. Yes. Duly noted."

Chapter Twenty-Four

Paris is Worth a Mass

rose early the next morning and prepared myself to spend the day cloistered in the Church of the Immaculate Conception, ready to pounce on Gorgiano when he came to kill General Cambon. I was surprised that Holmes was not already up and waiting for me at the breakfast table, but at half-past seven he joined me.

"Shall we catch a cab to Knightsbridge at eight?" I asked him.

"What for?"

"Aren't we going to accompany the Ambassador as he walks from his Embassy to the church?"

"We are. He will depart after ten o'clock."

"I thought he agreed to spend the whole day in prayer. He won't get started until eleven. A *day* doesn't start at eleven."

"He's French. The Almighty will have to wait. Have another cup of coffee."

At a quarter past ten, Holmes and I were huddled in a copse of trees on South Carriage Drive, where we had a full view of the porticoed entrance of the Embassy of France. The Ambassador emerged, accompanied by three large men who I hoped were armed guards. We followed them at a discreet distance as they walked east to the corner of the park and then turned up Park Lane toward Mayfair.

I kept scanning the view in every direction as we progressed toward Mount Street Gardens and the Church of the Immaculate Conception, expecting Gaetano Gorgiano to leap out from behind a tree or drop from a window at any moment.

He did not appear.

We watched as the four of them entered the church from a door at the back of the Lady chapel, and then we entered along with a small group of worshippers coming for morning Mass.

"This way," said Holmes, and I followed him up a narrow staircase to the choir loft that was situated in a balcony above the back of the nave.

General Cambon and his men sat in a pew behind most of the congregation and rose and knelt as directed by the Mass. Holmes had taken out his spyglass and trained it on each of those present and then handed it to me to do the same.

There was no sight of Gorgiano.

Mass ended, and the worshippers departed, leaving our three men and the priest. The Frenchmen slid out of their pews and moved toward the front of the church, where Father Ignatius greeted them and gestured to the closest pew to the altar. General Cambon entered and knelt, and his guards turned and pretended to leave the building. At least I hoped they pretended. Otherwise, he was left with no protection. He was a sitting duck, alone and immediately beside the center aisle.

I whispered my worry to Holmes.

"It is all right," he whispered back. "His guards will be hidden in the side chapels. Lestrade has his men hiding here as well."

After a brief five minutes, Father Ignatius appeared, walked slowly over to the General, made the sign of the cross over him, and placed an opened portfolio in front of him. General Cambon started reading it and turned the pages slowly.

"What is he doing?" I asked Holmes. "Did they prepare prayers for him to read?"

"Good heavens, no. God got his five minutes. He had his dispatches, a draft of the proposed treaty with England, and his briefings for the week all assembled to look like prayer portfolios."

I had underestimated French efficiency.

For a full hour after the Mass had ended, no one else entered the church, and our man continued to read and appeared to pray alone and in silence. At half-past one, he rose and started to walk down the nave to the main door.

"Is he done?" I asked.

"No. It's lunchtime. The Coburg Hotel is only a block away and has a superb French restaurant."

"Splendid. I could fancy a plate of *escargots* and some *coq au vin* myself."

"We're not going there. It would be too conspicuous. There is a cafe around the corner. You can enjoy something French there."

"What can a cafe serve me that's *French*?"

"Toast."

General Cambon finished his lunch an hour later, returned to the church and resumed his ostensible orisons. Except for a few elderly women who came in, knelt well back from the altar, prayed their rosaries, and departed, there was no activity.

The bell in the bell-tower was sounding out three o'clock when a man entered the church and walked directly to General Cambon. Holmes quickly pulled out his spyglass and then put it back.

"Some scribbler from Fleet Street who thinks he can get a story to print about the general. This should be amusing."

We could not hear what was being said, but the general waved the reporter off with a gesture of dismissal. The reporter ignored him and appeared to continue to ask questions. General Cambon finally closed his prayer book and stood up.

In a flash, his right arm swept across the space between the two men. The back of his hand struck the reporter hard in the face, and he fell back into the pews on the other side of the aisle. When he staggered back to his feet, the general was approaching him with his walking stick raised. The reporter, with blood streaming down his face, turned and ran out of the church.

"He can't assault a man like that," I said to Holmes. "It's against the law no matter how justified. He could be arrested for striking him."

"Diplomatic immunity," said Holmes.

At four o'clock, a spoken Mass was scheduled, and about twenty or so people entered and took places scattered throughout the sanctuary. I watched them closely, as did Holmes. Just before the priest entered to kiss the altar, a large-bodied, tall man entered and sat behind the rest of the worshippers. Holmes pulled out his spyglass and studied him carefully.

"It's him," he whispered. He leaned forward to the balcony rail and made a gesture with his hand to alert the constable and guards who were in hiding.

"Are you sure?"

"No. He is in disguise, but what I can see of his frame and facial features fit the images I have seen of Gorgiano."

"Can they jump him?"

"We promised the Jesuits we would not disturb a Mass. He will be accosted as he leaves when the service is over."

I waited and watched. The man we assumed was Gorgiano kept glancing around the sanctuary as the Mass progressed. At the end of the Eucharistic prayers, the congregation rose and began to work their way up the aisle to the altar rail. Gorgiano and stood and joined them. I felt Holmes's hand on my arm and could see that he was gesturing vigorously with his other.

"He's going to pass right past the Ambassador," he said. "This will be his chance."

"Where are the guards?"

"They are scattered through the congregation and hiding behind the altar. They'll be on him in more than enough time."

Gorgiano shuffled forward in the line to the altar rail and kept looking around as he did so. He was within twenty feet of the kneeling General Cambon when he quickly turned around and sprinted toward the back of the church. Holmes leapt to his feet and ran toward the staircase.

I followed him down, and we entered the narthex. Two constables and one of General Cambon's guards were already there, but there was no sign of the killer.

In what resembled a scene of comic relief, the police and the guards kept shouting, "He went that way ...No, he went *that* way... No, he ran out toward Mount Street."

It did not matter. He was gone.

I put my hand on Holmes's shoulder, certain that he must be feeling profound frustrated and discouraged.

"You came close. You'll get him next time."

"I suspect that he planned it carefully. It was a blind."

"What? He came within a minute of shooting him."

"No. He was not going to shoot him in the middle of a Mass. There are too many people around. He needed an empty church and at least twenty minutes to perform the dismemberment. He thinks he has fooled us."

"So, what now?"

"We follow the Ambassador back to the Embassy and then to his residence."

"You think he will try again?"

"I am reasonably certain that something will happen. Come."

Chapter Twenty-Five

We Hide in the Shrubbery

As he departed the church, General Cambon's guards joined him, and they walked back to the French Embassy. We followed at a distance. Being late November, darkness had already fallen, and we struggled to watch for any reappearance of Gorgiano.

The walk back was without incident. Ten minutes later, the general re-emerged from the Embassy and started walking west on Knightsbridge Road, and a block later cut off to the left and walked quickly along the pavement of Brompton Road. He stopped at an elegant house that sat back from the curb and was surrounded by a black, wrought-iron fence and a narrow garden.

"This," said Holmes, "is the residence of the French Ambassador. Come, we can watch from one of the windows."

"Holmes, are you sure—"

"Completely. Come."

On reaching the fence, he turned to me. "Put your hands together and let me use them as a step. And then give me a boost over the top."

I did just that, and then he returned the action by slipping his hand back through the fence and offering me the same help getting up and over. Once we were both on the ground, he edged his way through some shrubs until we were up against the wall and under one of the windows of the parlor. On my tiptoes, I was able to peer into the room.

It occurred to me that what we were doing might not be entirely legal, and at the very least, we could be taken into custody as Peeping Toms. Holmes clearly had no such qualms.

As we watched, General Cambon entered the room and took what appeared to be an office desk chair on casters by the top rail. He wheeled it in front of the hearth, and then he turned and approached the windows. One after the other, he pulled the drapes closed. As he approached the window through which we were peeking, we ducked to remain out of sight. The drapes closed, eliminating our view.

"Well," I said, "that puts paid to that effort."

"Just wait," Holmes replied.

I did, and about five minutes later, our drapes re-opened. The view was not entirely clear, but it looked as if the general was sitting in the wheeled chair, pushing himself around the room to the various windows and opening the drapes. Without getting up, he finally slid back in front of the hearth and seemed to be contentedly peering into the flickering hearth.

"Holmes?"

"Sssshh. Now, whatever you see or hear, do not make a sound. Keep silent no matter what."

I was in a complete fog, but I nodded and said nothing. Holmes took out his composite knife and very gently levered the sash window up by half an inch. A warm draft of air escaped, and he put his ear to the small slit of an opening. I could see no reason for not doing the same thing, even if I could see no reason for doing so. I tried to listen as well.

We waited in silence. The general sat still in his chair, only nodding or moving his head an inch or two from side to side. After about six minutes, a young blonde maid entered, wearing the uniform of a French maid that decent English families considered scandalous. She was bearing a small tray on which was perched a plate of cheese and a small glass filled with some sort of bright red liquor.

"*Votre apertif, votre Excellence.*"

"*Laissez-le sur la table.*"

She put the glass and the tray down of the coffee table. Having done so, she walked quickly up behind the general and extracted a small revolver from her bosom whilst doing so. I almost screamed a warning to him, but Holmes slapped his hand across my mouth.

The maid brought the gun up against the back of the general's head and fired. I watch in utter horror as his body jerked forward out of the chair and flopped onto the stone apron of the hearth. The butler, a young red-haired man, came charging into the room, and I fully expected that he would receive a bullet in his chest for his troubles.

To my stunned amazement, he dropped to his knees beside the body and pulled the right arm out until it was fully extended. He brought the white-gloved hand toward himself, and using a scalpel that he had been holding in his right hand, he started to cut into the wrist. Then he jumped back.

"*È falso! È una trappola. Corri adesso!*"

Neither of them got far. The general jumped out from behind a curtain and brought his stick down hard on the wrist of the maid, forcing her to drop the gun. Three constables and Inspector Lestrade rushed in from the back of the house and laid strong hands on the two of them.

Holmes leapt out of the shrubbery and ran to the front door with me at his heels. He rushed into the parlor and was met with the angry glares of the butler and the maid. He walked up to them and, first one then the other, removed their wigs. Tito and Michelina were glaring back at him.

"Adwa?" asked Holmes.

After a brief moment of silence, Dr. Lucheni answered.

"Si. Adwa."

"Your family?"

"Si. Nine of us. An eye for an eye."

The constables put the two of them in handcuffs and led them out of the house. A police wagon rolled up to the door, and they were taken away.

"My Campari is excellent, gentlemen," said the general, picking his apertif up off the coffee table. "Will you join me?"

Chapter Twenty-Six

In a Corner of the Dark Continent

With the constables and guards having departed, Lestrade, General Cambon, Holmes and I relaxed in the lavish parlor of the Ambassador's residence.

"All right, Holmes," said Lestrade as we sipped Campari. "Just what in the blazes is *Adwa,* and how did you know it was the Luchenis, and where, by the way, is Gorgiano? Start talking."

"Adwa is in Africa, gentlemen," said Holmes. "The north-east of Abyssinia, to be more precise. It is the only place in all of Africa where the Italian army ever engaged in direct battle and the only time that France, Russia and Abyssinia colluded to oppose the Italian Army. Italy was late to the game of claiming colonies in the Dark Continent, and by the time they got around to it, the only parts left unclaimed by the European powers were Eritrea and Abyssinia. The Italians established a colony in Eritrea and then, three years ago, attempted to march into Abyssinia and take it over. They only made it as far as Adwa."

"So, what happened there?" asked Lestrade.

"The Abyssinians were waiting for them. Eighty thousand of them, fully equipped with artillery and rifles and well-trained. The ten thousand Italians walked into a trap and were cut to ribbons. Half of them were killed or captured."

"Including Doctor and Michelina Lucheni?" I asked.

"I suspect so. They were a military family, and quite a few of them most likely were present at the battle. The Abyssinians were rather nasty to many of the prisoners and cut off a hand and foot of over three hundred of them. The Luchenis were driven by a furious desire for revenge, a *mad* desire for revenge. An eye for an eye became a hand and foot for a hand and foot."

"But how," asked Lestrade, "did those Africans manage to beat them? The Italians may not have a reputation for being the most fearsome of soldiers, but they were a modern European army fighting a bunch of natives with spears and arrows."

"Not quite, Inspector. But I will defer to General Cambon to answer that one. Your Excellency?"

The general took a slow sip of Campari and replied.

"*C'était facile.* Neither we nor the Russians and certainly not the Abyssinians wanted Italy to have control of the Horn of Africa and control access to the Suez. *Alors,* we and the Russians trained them and provided them with excellent French rifles, and ammunition. The Russians gave them artillery, and we both provided military advice. Both General Rainey and I directed the rapid training of over eighty thousand men. They may not have been the most hardened fighting force, but they were defending their homeland. That always makes for a fierce soldier."

"And the Russian?" asked Holmes.

"*Mais oui.* Count Nilolay Stepanovich Leontev was a very experienced military man and provided excellent advice. He arranged for the forty artillery pieces to be delivered."

"And the others?"

"Monsieur Routhier is the owner and manager of the factory that made the French rifles. Captain Guyse was a captain in the merchant marine and moved our arms and military advisors through the Suez and to French Somaliland. All of us who Dr. Lucheni came after were involved in some way in that battle."

"But why," I asked, "provide the list of names of the intended victims?"

The general shrugged and Holmes offered a reply. "To let them know that they were about to be murdered and dismembered, perhaps? To make them live in terror until their killer came for them? Who can say?"

"Where then," asked Lestrade, "does this Gorgiano fellow fit in? Did he not kill any of them?"

"It was simply a case of one Neapolitan making an agreement with another," said Holmes.

"Neapolitan?" I said. "The Luchenis were from the north of Italy. From Milan."

"So, they tried to lead us to believe. No, they were also from Naples."

"How did you know that?"

"Elementary. The first hint was when Michelina served us *ciambelle* and *limoncello*. Neither of those is from the North. They are southern. My suspicions were confirmed when we had dinner together. The wine I ordered and the *primo, secondo* and *dolce* plates they requested were all favorites of the Neapolitans but almost unknown north of Rome."

"Are you saying," I asked, "that they colluded and helped him escape?"

"Yes. They made an agreement, sealed with a handshake. The Luchenis helped Gorgiano escape from a lifetime in Broadmoor by letting him slip into the medical supplies carriage. In return, he did not have to kill anyone himself, but he had to be willing to have himself identified as the killer. Once the acts of revenge were complete, he would be free to escape, likely back to America. That was their agreement, and neither the military families of Naples nor the *Camorra* will ever betray a promise to another son of Naples."

"Who did the killing?" asked Lestrade.

"Michelina mostly. As a nurse who served in a military hospital, she did not flinch from blood or death. It was she, as a beautiful young woman who, unsuspected, was able to come up behind General Thierry in his bedroom. It was the two of them who each fired a shot in the home of the Russian. And it was the doctor who knew how to rapidly amputate a hand or a foot. Dr. Watson will attest that it is a skill that, tragically, is necessary to acquire when serving on the battlefront."

"*Je crois que c'est tout,*" said the general. "Another round of Campari, *mes amies*?"

He stood, picked up the bottle, and started to make the rounds when we heard the front door of the residence open. A moment later, a large man with a rubicund complexion stood in the doorway. He was holding a revolver in each hand, and they were pointed at us.

Chapter Twenty-Seven

The Handsome Blond Eyesore

"Hey there fellas. Thought I should drop by and say *ciao*. Been nice getting to know you. Real sorry about dropping you into the vat, Mr. Holmes, but it had to be done. An agreement is an agreement."

"Mr. Gaetano Gorgiano, I presume?" said Holmes, although there was no question as to who it was we were looking at.

"That's me. Followed you fellas here and saw what all happened. Got to hand it to you. That was real smart. Tricked the Luchenis into coming here instead. Now relax. I'm not here to hurt anyone. I coulda just vanished, but I had to make one thing clear before I leave. You and the Luchenis gotta know that I kept up my part of the agreement. You didn't learn nothing from me. I never betrayed nobody. That's clear. Right? I don't want it going around Naples that I was a traitor to my people."

"Your peculiar brand of honor," said Holmes, "has not been besmirched."

"Hey, that's good. Now you fellas take care of yourselves. It's got kinda hot for me here in London, so I'm going back to the good old U S of A. *Ciao.*"

He turned, and in a few strides of his long legs, he was out of the house. Lestrade rushed after him in time to see him hop into a waiting carriage and vanish along Cromwell Street.

The four of us returned to our chairs and looked at each other without saying anything and without sipping any more Campari. Finally, Lestrade sighed.

"Right. Looks like that's over. We'll let the Americans know, and maybe the Pinkerton men can find him. Well now, Holmes, what about this idea of yours that there was a second killer who attacked the girl?"

"One item at a time," said Holmes. "It was necessary to remove these two first. Tomorrow, I shall attempt to find and eliminate the *peculiar* second killer."

"Right. Then I guess we can have a drink to that," said Lestrade as he lifted his glass to his lips. He did not get a chance to imbibe. A constable came barging into the house and crashed into the room.

"Inspector, sir!"

"Good grief, man, what is it?"

"That Gorgiano killer. He's struck again."

"When? Where?"

"Just in the last hour."

"Impossible. He was following us, and then he was here."

The constable looked utterly confused.

"Well, sir, somebody attacked another girl from Queen's Gate."

I gasped in horror, and I could see Holmes's face turn pale.

Holmes, Lestrade and I leapt to our feet to follow the constable out to the waiting police carriage. I looked back at General Cambon to see if he was coming with us.

"*Je n'ai pas de chien dans ce combat,*" he said and gave a Gallic shrug.

The carriage raced south through Kensington and Chelsea toward the Embankment.

"Where are we going?" Holmes asked the constable. He spoke softly. I could hear the despair in his voice.

"Scotland Yard, sir."

"Why there? Surely, that is not where the crime was committed."

"Don't ask me, sir. I was just told to go and find the inspector and get him back to the Yard, and if Mr. Holmes was with him, to bring him along."

We arrived at Scotland Yard within ten minutes and hurried into the entry hall.

"We got him, Inspector!" shouted one of the constables at the desk. "We got him."

"Got who?" demanded Lestrade.

"The killer. The one what cut up the girl."

"Is he in one of the cells?"

"No, sir. He's in the morgue. Quite dead he is. C'mon. I'll show you."

We descended to the morgue. Lying on a slab was the body of an exceptionally handsome young man. He had aristocratic facial features and blond hair. One side of his face was covered in blood. The cause was obvious. He had an expensive stiletto with a gold and Mother-of-Pearl handle lodged in his eye socket."

"As you can see, Inspector. He's as dead as they come."

"Crikey," said Lestrade. "This chap is a dead ringer, if you will pardon the expression, for the demented bloke we sent off to Broadmoor a few years ago. Do you remember him, Holmes?"

Holmes started to nod and then stopped. He looked at the corpse for a full minute and said, "I do remember that case, but it was not this fellow. Only one who looked like him. Is this the one who killed the girl?"

"Oh no, sir," said the constable. "The girl's alive. A bit roughed up but still alive."

I was stunned, and I heard Holmes utter what, for him, passed as a prayer of thanks to the Almighty.

"Where is she?" said Lestrade.

"Up in the interrogation room. Has her headmistress with her."

Chapter Twenty-Eight

The School Rules are Broken

Seated on uncomfortable hard chairs in one of the smaller rooms was the headmistress of Queen's Gate School, Miss Wyatt. Beside her, slouching back into the chair and stretching her long legs into the room, was an exceptionally attractive young woman dressed in a school uniform. Even in that garb and with bruises and scratches on her face, she looked quintessentially French.

I remembered her from the schoolyard, and I assumed that she must have been the victim of the attack.

As Holmes entered, I could see the look of relief pass over his countenance. He sat in one of the chairs and, as was his custom in such a situation, he took out his cigarette case and lit one.

The girl stood, walked over to Holmes, reached out her hand and took the cigarette out of his. She returned to her chair and began to puff away on it.

"Gabrielle," said Headmistress Wyatt. "You know the rules of our school."

With the look of disdain that only a beautiful French woman can get away with, she said, "A man tried to rape me and murder me. I had to kill him. I will enjoy a cigarette. *Tais-toi ...s'il vous plaît.*"

Lestrade was nonplussed but managed to recover and start his questions.

"Miss Gabrielle Cartier ... is that your name?"

"*Oui.*"

"I know it is difficult, but can you please tell us what happened this evening?"

"*Ce n'est pas difficile,*" she said and took another languorous draft on the cigarette.

"Right, well then, tell us anyway."

I observed the second Gallic shrug of that evening.

"I was marching through our schoolyard on my way to the home of the people I board with. A man was coming toward me, and he called out my name. I was surprised but assumed that he must know me, so I stopped to chat. He was a *beau jeune homme,* and he came close to me and offered me a cigarette. *Alors,* I talked to him. But then he started to say things that were rude about my *croupe.* How do you say it? My arse. And about my breasts. And then he grabbed me and tried to kiss me. I was not afraid. Men in Paris do this all the time to young women."

"You *let* him kiss you?" said Lestrade.

Another shrug. "He gave me a cigarette. I gave him a kiss. This is fair, *oui*?"

"Uh...right, continue."

"Then he became very strange. He said he was going to do to me what he had done to my friend, Celestine. That was when I knew that he was not just a young man who wanted to flirt. I thought that he might be the man who killed her, but I could not be sure. So, I let him kiss me again. While he was doing so, he ripped my blouse open and touched me in a way he should not. I could see that he had a knife in his hand. Miss Wyatt had given all of us French girls these lovely little *armes.* What do you call them? Stilettos? I kissed him, which surprised him, and while doing so, I took out the knife and pushed it very hard into his eye. He screamed and staggered back and called me names and died. What more is there to tell?"

We looked at her in something approaching disbelief and awe.

"Nothing that I can think of right now," said Lestrade. "How about you, Holmes?"

He shook his head.

"Well then, young lady, I guess you can go back to the house you live in. *C'est tout, n'est-ce pas.* Isn't that what they say in France?"

Miss Gabrielle took another puff on her cigarette. "Please, sir, do not try to speak French."

"I am rather hungry," said Holmes when the two of us were out of Scotland Yard. "Would you fancy dinner at Simpson's? It is not far from here."

"Does this mean that we are celebrating the successful conclusion of the case?" I asked.

"Not yet. We have to pay one more visit to Broadmoor tomorrow."

Chapter Twenty-Nine

The Puzzle is Revealed

Early the next morning, we again caught the train from Paddington to Reading and from there on to Crowthorne. Both of us settled in and read both the morning papers and a couple from the previous evening that we had missed as a result of other priorities.

The news of the arrest of the Luchenis had not yet been released by Scotland Yard, but there was yet another article in the *Evening Star* by the reporter, Devin Brewster, on the conditions in Broadmoor. Again, he provided information on several of the patients and the staff that was considered highly confidential, and again he—rather self-righteously as far as I was concerned—lambasted the administration for the easy escape of the monster, Big Red Gorgiano.

"A shame," I said to Holmes, "that you couldn't add this charlatan to your investigation. He has no respect whatsoever for the privacy of either the patients or the staff, and his claims border on outright lies."

"Every occupation has a few members who are beneath contempt. Fortunately, the great majority of the Press have some sense of honesty and decency. As for this vile character, his comeuppance may arrive sooner rather than later."

He took the newspaper from me and stuffed it into a valise that was already filled with other copies of the same newspaper.

"Is anyone expecting us?" I asked Holmes as we approached the massive walls and gated entry of the hospital.

"During the night, I sent off a telegram to the director. There has not been time for a reply, but I expect that the contents will be sufficient for him to welcome us."

"What did you tell him?"

"That the doctor and nurse whom he selected and hired had committed multiple murders, and I was investigating the possibility that other members of his staff were so inclined."

"Well, that should get his attention."

At the gates, we were again greeted by Virgil Bolton, who had not been apprised of our visit but appeared pleased to see us. He led us to the office of the director of the hospital.

"Your visit, Mr. Holmes," said Bolton, "must be important if you have to see Doc Pollard."

"It is," said Holmes, "and I will be asking him if, in addition to having you serve as our guide, we might also have your continuing services this morning to protect us."

"You are? What for?"

"I will be requesting a face-to-face meeting with Archibald Castellucci."

Bolton let out a low whistle. "You will need protection. He's as unpredictable as he is evil and wild. No telling what he might do. But for sure, I'll be happy to come along. I almost would not mind if he tried something. It would give me an excuse to let him have it."

"Now, now. We'll have none of that, young man," said Holmes, and he gave Bolton a friendly pat on the shoulder.

Doc Pollard shooed some other officials out of his office when we arrived at his door and welcomed us. He had by now received confirmation that his doctor and nurse had been arrested and that Gaetano Gorgiano had escaped the clutches of the police one more time. Added to that, yet another smear in the Press, and he was already having a very bad day.

"If you find anything else amiss, Mr. Holmes, I would be most grateful if you could let me know. My staff here are awfully demoralized by what has happened and by the horrible lies being told in that newspaper. And please, if you can still continue to try and find Gorgiano, that would be splendid."

"I suspect," said Holmes, "that he is already on his way to America. I suggest that you hire Mr. Iwan of Pinkertons to follow him, find him, and bring him back. He is quite a capable fellow."

"I will do that. And do I understand correctly that you think there may be some connection between the murders and Archibald Castellucci?"

"Possibly. I will let you know after we meet with him."

"Quite so, sir. Bolton here will stay with you. Do you want anyone else to accompany you?"

"Yes. Mr. John Shepherd."

"Him? Our archivist and records man? What in the world for?"

"He has read every report on every patient here for the past twenty years. He knows them all, including both Castellucci and Gorgiano, better than anyone else. He will be invaluable."

"If you say so, Mr. Holmes. You can blow on your police whistle if there are problems, and more guards will be there on the double. This Castellucci chap is a true lunatic."

From the director's office, we hurried over to the Records and Archive Room and fetched Mr. Shepherd.

"Your close observations of the reports on this mad man," said Holmes, "were most useful. Please be prepared to observe everything you can during our meeting and let me know if anything else seems out of order."

"I can tell you now," he said, "that the contents of the reports on this fellow over the past three weeks have been strange."

"Indeed? Is he becoming even more dangerous?"

"No, and that's the strange thing. Before, he was quiet and sullen, and the way he looked at members of the staff was enough for them to be terrified. Now he bellows, but those who meet with him do not find him at all frightening, merely objectionable and belligerent."

When the door to the room of Archibald Castellucci was unlocked and opened and we entered, all the confusing parts of this puzzle fell into place.

Chapter Thirty

If There Is Any Justice

The man I was looking at bore an uncanny resemblance to the corpse I had observed the previous evening. If I had not known otherwise, I would have sworn they were twin brothers.

As soon as the four of us entered his room, he leapt to his feet and began to curse and shout and wave his arms. His threats were colorful and creative, if not at all believable. He struck me as more like an annoying schoolboy having a temper tantrum than a criminal lunatic.

"Mr. Bolton," said Holmes, "would you be so kind as to help Mr. Castellucci settle down?"

Virgil Bolton stepped forward and delivered a haymaker to the face of Mr. Castellucci. He fell backwards on to his bed, looking completely stunned.

"You can't do that! I'll get you for that, Bolton. I know who you are and where you live. As soon as I get out of here, I'll get even with you. Just you watch. I'll make you hated all over England."

"Your threats, sir," said Holmes, "are quite intriguing. Here. Let me help you with a few ideas of how you might write something in a newspaper to falsely smear the good name of Mr. Bolton."

He opened his valise and took out the bundle of *Evening Star* newspapers. They had all been opened to the third page, and Holmes began to read out loud the first paragraphs of the sequence of articles written by Devin Brewster. As he did, a smug smile spread across the face of the man sitting on the bed, smirking at us.

"Well, well, well. The great detective, Mr. Sherlock Holmes, took his sweet time seeing through my brilliant disguise. I would not have minded if it had gone for another fortnight, but for three weeks, it's been a great ride. Can't beat that, now can you? A featured byline every four days. Drove our circulation up by over ten thousand. Bloody brilliant, if I do say so."

"Does your editor know about your .... your *brilliant disguise*?"

"Of course not. How naive do you think I am? My editor is smart enough not to ask, and I'm smart enough not to tell."

"Would you like to brag, Mr. ... Castellucci, about how you pulled it off?"

He shrugged. "Yeah. May as well now. Worked perfectly. Brilliant, if I do say to. A couple of months ago, someone told me that my resemblance to some crazy killer in Broadmoor was beyond belief. I smelled the possibility of some exclusive stories and came and met with the mad man. Couldn't believe how much we looked like each other. I made a deal with him, and he jumped at the chance."

"What you mean," said Holmes, "is that you broke the law and offered to change clothes with him and let him walk out of the hospital pretending he was you and let you stay inside so you could write your stories."

"Law, schmaw. If I got arrested, all I had to do is swear that he had knocked me out. Stripped me and changed clothes and then threatened that he would carve up my family unless I let him escape for at least a month. My paper has some great lawyers. If it came to court, we would plead that we had no choice. I'd get away with a slap on the wrist or a fine at the worst."

"You are aware though," said Holmes, "that the man you let escape viciously killed one young woman and attacked another and is now dead himself. Their blood is on your hands, is it not?"

"Not my problem. If the school cannot provide protection for their students, that's their fault. If Scotland Yard cannot stop a crazy killer, that's their problem. As soon as you leave, I'll call the director and drop my disguise and get out of here. Just watch, mister great detective."

"Will you now?" said Holmes. "Well then, allow me to bid you good day and may your body rot in this cell and your soul in Hell, Mr. Castellucci."

Holmes rose, and we followed him out of the room.

"Hey, don't be a poor loser," the reporter shouted after us. "And you better start calling me by my real name if you don't want to look like a complete dupe."

The door of the room was locked behind us. Holmes stopped once we were back outside and had a brief chat with the three of us. Smiles of righteous satisfaction spread across our faces. We proceeded to the office of the director.

"Did you find out anything?" asked the director. "Can that Castellucci chap help lead us to Gorgiano?"

"I fear not," said Holmes. "However, I fear that your patient has taken a turn for the worse. He has become infinitely more dangerous than before."

"Oh dear. In what way?"

"He is making threats against members of the staff of the hospital, including yourself, as well as against members of the public, including Her Majesty. If he were ever to escape, the results would be horrible."

"Good lord. We can't let that happen. I'll make sure he is guarded around the clock."

"He has also become not only utterly evil, he is obviously delusional. He is now making claims that he is not in fact Archibald Castellucci, the crazed killer, but a certain Devin Brewster of the *Evening Star,* a reporter to whom he has a singular physical resemblance."

"Him? You mean that reporter who keeps writing those lies about us?"

"Precisely. I believe you will find that he made several visits to the hospital a few weeks back and met with Castellucci. It may well be that Castellucci has been the source of the confidential information that Brewster has published."

"I'll put a stop to that right away. No more visitors."

"A capital idea, Doctor. The four of us also admit that he almost persuaded us, but that we could see that he was beyond pretending. He truly believed himself to be someone other than who he truly was. As such, he is infinitely more dangerous than before. Far be it from us to say how he should be treated, but we suggest, sir, that unless you wish your good name and that of the hospital to be dragged through the mud yet again, you would be wise to keep him in solitary confinement and not allow anyone from the public to visit with him until such time and he ceases to exhibit his delusions."

"I'll take your advice and recommendations under advisement, and I thank you, sir. You've saved me and the hospital another setback in our efforts to treat those who are sick and mad in their minds. We won't let this Castellucci chap do any more harm than he has already done."

Holmes and I stood outside the gates and walls of Broadmoor, looking back at it.

"Will it work?" I asked him.

He lit a cigarette and stared back at the gates for at least a minute.

"He did say that no one, not even his editor, knew about his brilliant deception, did he not?"

"He did."

"Excellent. Then his next story, his *last,* will be submitted to his editor, claiming that he is hot on the trail of the murderous Big Red Gorgiano and is about to courageously confront him. Yes, that should do."

"But he's not going to write *that.*"

"No, Watson. You will."

"Oh."

"Mr. Bolton and Mr. Shepherd will adjust the reports as required, noting that he continues to scream about the horrible murders he plans to commit. The *Pall Mall Gazette* will run an exclusive story about Gorgiano's escape and his boasting about blowing the brains out of a pesky reporter and dumping him in the Thames. Yes, that should not be difficult. You will send the anonymous letter to Mr. Straight. If Lestrade will cooperate, and I believe he will, and have the real Castellucci buried in the Potter's Field as an unidentified murderer, there is a good chance that Mr. Brewster will be incarcerated here for at least a year, maybe two. If there is any justice in the world, possibly much longer."

"Good."

Did you enjoy this story? Are there ways it could have been improved? Please help the author and future readers of New Sherlock Holmes Mysteries by submitting a constructive review on the site from which you purchased it. Thank you. Very much appreciated. CSC

Dear Sherlockian Readers:

We have come a long way in our treatment of the mentally ill. The St. Mary Bethlehem Hospital—later known as Bethlem or Bedlam—was opened and starting housing the 'insane' in the 1300s and continues to do so to this day. In the 1860s, the government of the UK recognized a need for an institution to treat those who committed criminal acts but who were not criminally responsible. The Criminal Lunatic Asylum in Broadmoor opened in 1863 and continues to provide care and treatment for those sent there by the courts. The descriptions of it in this story are more or less accurate for the time. Corrections from readers are welcomed.

The Italians came late to the 'scramble for Africa' and the only foothold they secured was in the Horn of Africa. They established a colony in Eritrea during the 1880s. Visitors to Asmara today often remark on how much it resembles Sienna. In 1896, Italy attempted to extend their colonial possessions by advancing into Abyssinia (now known as Ethiopia). The Abyssinians banded together to resist them and received extensive military aid, armaments and advice from both the French and the Russians, as recounted in this story.

At the battle of Adwa, the advancing Italian force met an overwhelming Abyssinian army and lost badly. Many of the captives were tortured in the manner described in the story.

The passing reference to Winston Churchill is accurate.

The *Camorra* originated in Naples and extended their criminal activities and influence throughout the UK, parts of Europe, and the US. They were distinct from the Mafia, who originated in Sicily. The reference to Giuseppe 'Black" Gorgiano is taken from *The Adventure of the Red Circle.*

Pinkerton's Detective Agency was formed in 1855 in Chicago and has provided private security services to countless clients since then. The concept of the 'private eye' originated with their early accomplishments. You can Google them if you want to know more.

The names of places in London and the surrounding counties are generally accurate for 1899. Goldini's, a 'garish Italian restaurant,' is borrowed from *The Adventure of the Bruce-Partington Plans.* Simpson's-in-the-Strand is said to be the favorite restaurant of Sherlock Holmes based on its being mentioned twice in The Canon. I've been there. It's still really good.

The French Embassy today is located on Knightsbridge. Not sure if it was there in 1899. If you know, please tell me.

Warm regards. Happy sleuthing and deducing,   Craig

.

About the Author

In May of 2014, the Sherlock Holmes Society of Canada – better known as The Bootmakers – announced a contest for a new Sherlock Holmes story. Although he had no experience writing fiction, the author submitted a short Sherlock Holmes mystery and was blessed to be declared one of the winners. Thus inspired, he has continued to write new Sherlock Holmes Mysteries since and is on a mission to write a new story as a tribute to each of the sixty stories in the original Canon. He has been writing stories while living in Tokyo, Buenos Aires, Bahrain, Toronto, the Okanagan, and New York City. Several readers of New Sherlock Holmes Mysteries have kindly sent him suggestions for future stories. You are welcome to do likewise at: craigstephencopland@gmail.com.

More Historical Mysteries
by Craig Stephen Copland

www.SherlockHolmesMystery.com

Follow links to look inside and download

Studying Scarlet. Starlet O'Halloran, a fabulous mature woman, who reminds the reader of Scarlet O'Hara (but who, for copyright reasons cannot actually be her) has arrived in London looking for her long-lost husband, Brett (who resembles Rhett Butler, but who, for copyright reasons, cannot actually be him). She enlists the help of Sherlock Holmes. This is an unauthorized parody, inspired by Arthur Conan Doyle's *A Study in Scarlet* and Margaret Mitchell's *Gone with the Wind.*

The Sign of the Third. Fifteen hundred years ago, the courageous Princess Hemamali smuggled the sacred tooth of the Buddha into Ceylon. Now, for the first time, it is being brought to London to be part of a magnificent exhibit at the British Museum. But what if something were to happen to it? It would be a disaster for the British Empire. Sherlock Holmes, Dr. Watson, and even Mycroft Holmes are called upon to prevent such a crisis. This novella is inspired by the Sherlock Holmes mystery, The Sign of the Four.

A Sandal from East Anglia. Archeological excavations at an old abbey unearth an ancient document that has the potential to change the course of the British Empire and all of Christendom. Holmes encounters some evil young men and a strikingly beautiful young Sister, with a curious double life. The mystery is inspired by the original Sherlock Holmes story, *A Scandal in Bohemia*

The Bald-Headed Trust. Watson insists on taking Sherlock Holmes on a short vacation to the seaside in Plymouth. No sooner has Holmes arrived than he is needed to solve a double murder and prevent a massive fraud diabolically designed by the evil Professor himself. Who knew that a family of devout conservative churchgoers could come to the aid of Sherlock Holmes and bring enormous grief to evildoers? The story is inspired by *The Red-Headed League.*

A Case of Identity Theft. It is the fall of 1888, and Jack the Ripper is terrorizing London. A young married couple is found, minus their heads. Sherlock Holmes, Dr. Watson, the couple's mothers, and Mycroft must join forces to find the murderer before he kills again and makes off with half a million pounds. The novella is a tribute to A Case of Identity. It will appeal both to devoted fans of Sherlock Holmes, as well as to those who love the great game of rugby

The Hudson Valley Mystery. A young man in New York went mad and murdered his father. His mother believes he is innocent and knows he is not crazy. She appeals to Sherlock Holmes and, together with Dr. and Mrs. Watson, he crosses the Atlantic to help this client in need. This new story was inspired by *The Boscombe Valley*

The Mystery of the Five Oranges. A desperate father enters 221B Baker Street. His daughter has been kidnapped and spirited off to North America. The evil network who have taken her has spies everywhere. There is only one hope – Sherlock Holmes. Sherlockians will enjoy this new adventure, inspired by The Five Orange Pips and Anne of Green Gables.

www.SherlockHolmesMystery.com

The Man Who Was Twisted But Hip. France is torn apart by The Dreyfus Affair. Westminster needs Sherlock Holmes so that the evil tide of anti-Semitism that has engulfed France will not spread. Sherlock and Watson go to Paris to solve the mystery and thwart Moriarty. This new mystery is inspired by *The Man with the Twisted Lip,* as well as by *The Hunchback of Notre Dame*

The Adventure of the Blue Belt Buckle. A young street urchin discovers a man's belt and buckle under a bush in Hyde Park. A body is found in a hotel room in Mayfair. Scotland Yard seeks the help of Sherlock Holmes in solving the murder. The Queen's Jubilee could be ruined. Sherlock Holmes, Dr. Watson, Scotland Yard, and Her Majesty all team up to prevent a crime of unspeakable dimensions. A new mystery inspired by *The Blue Carbuncle*. http://authl.it/aim

The Adventure of the Spectred Bat. A beautiful young woman, just weeks away from giving birth, arrives at Baker Street in the middle of the night. Her sister was attacked by a bat and died, and now it is attacking her. A vampire? The story is a tribute to *The Adventure of the Speckled Band* and, like the original, leaves the mind wondering and the heart racing. http://authl.it/ain

The Adventure of the Engineer's Mom. A brilliant young Cambridge University engineer is carrying out secret research for the Admiralty. It will lead to the building of the world's most powerful battleship, The Dreadnaught. His adventuress mother is kidnapped, and he seeks the help of Sherlock Holmes. This new mystery is a tribute to *The Engineer's Thumb*. http://authl.it/aio

www.SherlockHolmesMystery.com

150

The Adventure of the Notable Bachelorette. A snobbish nobleman enters 221B Baker Street, demanding the help in finding his much younger wife – a beautiful and spirited American from the West. Three days later, the wife is accused of a vile crime. Now she comes to Sherlock Holmes seeking to prove her innocence. This new mystery was inspired by *The Adventure of the Noble Bachelor.*

The Adventure of the Beryl Anarchists. A deeply distressed banker enters 221B Baker St. His safe has been robbed, and he is certain that his motorcycle-riding sons have betrayed him. Highly incriminating and embarrassing records of the financial and personal affairs of England's nobility are now in the hands of blackmailers. Then a young girl is murdered. A tribute to *The Adventure of the Beryl Coronet.*

The Adventure of the Coiffured Bitches. A beautiful young woman will soon inherit a lot of money. She disappears. Another young woman finds out far too much and, in desperation, seeks help. Sherlock Holmes, Dr. Watson, and Miss Violet Hunter must solve the mystery of the coiffured bitches and avoid the massive mastiff that could tear their throats out. A tribute to *The Adventure of the Copper Beeches*

The Silver Horse, Braised. The greatest horse race of the century will take place at Epsom Downs. Millions have been bet. Owners, jockeys, grooms, and gamblers from across England and America arrive. Jockeys and horses are killed. Holmes fails to solve the crime until… This mystery is a tribute to *Silver Blaze* and the great racetrack stories of Damon Runyon.

The Box of Cards. A brother and a sister from a strict religious family disappear. The parents are alarmed, but Scotland Yard says they are just off sowing their wild oats. A horrific, gruesome package arrives in the post, and it becomes clear that a terrible crime is in process. Sherlock Holmes is called in to help. A tribute to *The Cardboard Box*

The Yellow Farce. Sherlock Holmes is sent to Japan. The war between Russia and Japan is raging. Alliances between countries in these years before World War I are fragile, and any misstep could plunge the world into Armageddon. The wife of the British ambassador is suspected of being a Russian agent. Join Holmes and Watson as they travel around the world to Japan. Inspired by *The Yellow Face.*

The Stock Market Murders. A young man's friend has gone missing. Two more bodies of young men turn up. All are tied to The City and to one of the greatest frauds ever visited upon the citizens of England. The story is based on the true story of James Whitaker Wright and is inspired by *The Stock Broker's Clerk.* Any resemblance of the villain to a certain American political figure is entirely coincidental.

The Glorious Yacht. On the night of April 12, 1912, off the coast of Newfoundland, one of the greatest disasters of all time took place – the Unsinkable Titanic struck an iceberg and sank with a horrendous loss of life. The news of the disaster leads Holmes and Watson to reminisce about one of their earliest adventures. It began as a sailing race and ended as a tale of murder, kidnapping, piracy, and survival through a tempest. A tribute to *The Gloria Scott.*

www.SherlockHolmesMystery.com

A Most Grave Ritual. In 1649, King Charles I escaped and made a desperate run for Continent. Did he leave behind a vast fortune? The patriarch of an ancient Royalist family dies in the courtyard, and the locals believe that the headless ghost of the king did him in. The police accuse his son of murder. Sherlock Holmes is hired to exonerate the lad. A tribute to *The Musgrave Ritual*

The Spy Gate Liars. Dr. Watson receives an urgent telegram telling him that Sherlock Holmes is in France and near death. He rushes to aid his dear friend, only to find that what began as a doctor's housecall has turned into yet another adventure as Sherlock Holmes races to keep an unknown ruthless murderer from dispatching yet another former German army officer. A tribute to *The Reigate Squires.*

The Cuckold Man Colonel James Barclay needs the help of Sherlock Holmes. His exceptionally beautiful, but much younger, wife has disappeared, and foul play is suspected. Has she been kidnapped and held for ransom? Or is she in the clutches of a deviant monster? The story is a tribute not only to the original mystery, *The Crooked Man*, but also to the biblical story of King David and Bathsheba

The Impatient Dissidents. In March 1881, the Czar of Russia was assassinated by anarchists. That summer, an attempt was made to murder his daughter, Maria, the wife of England's Prince Alfred. A Russian Count is found dead in a hospital in London. Scotland Yard and the Home Office arrive at 221B and enlist the help of Sherlock Holmes to track down the killers and stop them. This new mystery is a tribute to *The Resident Patient.*

The Grecian, Earned. This story picks up where *The Greek Interpreter* left off. The villains of that story were murdered in Budapest, and so Holmes and Watson set off in search of "the Grecian girl" to solve the mystery. What they discover is a massive plot involving the re-birth of the Olympic games in 1896 and a colorful cast of characters at home and on the Continent.

The Three Rhodes Not Taken. Oxford University is famous for its passionate pursuit of learning. The Rhodes Scholarship has been recently established, and some men are prepared to lie, steal, slander, and, maybe murder, in the pursuit of it. Sherlock Holmes is called upon to track down a thief who has stolen vital documents pertaining to the winner of the scholarship, but what will he do when the prime suspect is found dead? A tribute to *The Three Students*

The Naval Knaves. On September 15, 1894, an anarchist attempted to bomb the Greenwich Observatory. He failed, but the attempt led Sherlock Holmes into an intricate web of spies, foreign naval officers, and a beautiful princess. Once again, suspicion landed on poor Percy Phelps, now working in a senior position in the Admiralty, and once again, Holmes has to use both his powers of deduction and raw courage to not only rescue Percy but to prevent an unspeakable disaster. A tribute to *The Naval Treaty.*

A Scandal in Trumplandia. NOT a new mystery but a political satire. The story is a parody of the much-loved original story, *A Scandal in Bohemia*, with the character of the King of Bohemia replaced by you-know-who. If you enjoy both political satire and Sherlock Holmes, you will get a chuckle out of this new story.

The Binomial Asteroid Problem. The deadly final encounter between Professor Moriarty and Sherlock Holmes took place at Reichenbach Falls. But when was their first encounter? This new story answers that question. What began a stolen Gladstone bag escalates into murder and more. This new story is a tribute to *The Adventure of the Final Problem.*

The Adventure of Charlotte Europa Golderton. *Charles Augustus Milverton* was shot and sent to his just reward. But now another diabolical scheme of blackmail has emerged centered in the telegraph offices of the Royal Mail. It is linked to an archeological expedition whose director disappeared. Someone is prepared to murder to protect their ill-gotten gain and possibly steal a priceless treasure. Holmes is hired by not one but three women who need his help.

The Mystery of 222 Baker Street. The body of a Scotland Yard inspector is found in a locked room in 222 Baker Street. There is no clue as to how he died. Then another murder in the very same room. Holmes and Watson might have to offer themselves as potential victims if the culprits are to be discovered. A tribute to the original Sherlock Holmes story, *The Adventure of the Empty House*

The Adventure of the Norwood Rembrandt. A man facing execution appeals to Sherlock Holmes to save him. He claims that he is innocent. Holmes agrees to take on his case. Five years ago, he was convicted of the largest theft of art masterpieces in British history, and of murdering the butler who tried to stop him. Holmes and Watson have to find the real murderer and the missing works of art --- if the client is innocent after all. A tribute to *The Adventure of the Norwood Builder* in the original Canon.

 ***The Horror of the Bastard's Villa.*** A Scottish clergyman and his faithful border collie visit 221B and tell a tale of a ghostly Banshee on the Isle of Skye. After the specter appeared, two people died. Holmes sends Watson on ahead to investigate and report. More terrifying horrors occur, and Sherlock Holmes must come and solve the awful mystery before more people are murdered. A tribute to the original story in the Canon, Arthur Conan Doyle's masterpiece, *The Hound of the Baskervilles* .

 ***The Dancer from the Dance.*** In 1909 the entire world of dance changed when Les Ballets Russes opened in Paris. They also made annual visits to the West End in London. Tragically, during their 1913 tour, two of their dancers are found murdered. Sherlock Holmes is brought into to find the murderer and prevent any more killings. The story adheres fairly closely to the history of ballet and is a tribute to the original story in the Canon, *The Adventure of the Dancing Men*.

 ***The Solitary Bicycle Thief***. Remember Violet Smith, the beautiful young woman whom Sherlock Holmes and Dr. Watson rescued from a forced marriage, as recorded in *The Adventure of the Solitary Cyclist*? Ten years later, she and Cyril reappear in 221B Baker Street with a strange tale of the theft of their bicycles. What on the surface seemed like a trifle turns out to be the door that leads Sherlock Holmes into a web of human trafficking, espionage, blackmail, and murder. A new and powerful cabal of master criminals has formed in London, and they will stop at nothing, not even the murder of an innocent foreign student, to extend the hold on the criminal underworld of London

www.SherlockHolmesMystery.com

The Adventure of the Prioress's Tale. The senior field hockey team from an elite girls' school goes to Dover for a beach holiday … and disappears. Have they been abducted into white slavery? Did they run off to Paris? Are they being held for ransom? Can Sherlock Holmes find them in time? Holmes, Watson, Lestrade, the Prioress of the school, and a new gang of Irregulars must find them before something terrible happens. a tribute to *The Adventure of the Priory School in the Canon.*

The Adventure of Mrs. J.L. Heber. A mad woman is murdering London bachelors by driving a railway spike through their heads. Scotland Yard demands that Sherlock Holmes help them find and stop a crazed murderess who is re-enacting the biblical murders by Jael. Holmes agrees and finds that revenge is being taken for deeds treachery and betrayal that took place ten years ago in the Rocky Mountains of Canada. Holmes, Watson, and Lestrade must move quickly before more men and women lose their lives. The story is a tribute to the original Sherlock Holmes story, *The Adventure of Black Peter.*

The Return of Napoleon. In October 1805, Napoleon's fleet was defeated in the Battle of Trafalgar. Now his ghost has returned to England for the centenary of the battle, intent on wreaking revenge on the descendants of Admiral Horatio Nelson and on all of England. The mother of the great-great-grandchildren of Admiral Nelson contacts Sherlock Holmes, needing his help. First, Dr. Watson comes to the manor, and he meets not only the lovely children but also finds that something apparently supernatural is going on. Holmes assumes that some mad Frenchmen, intent on avenging Napoleon, are conspiring to wreak havoc on England and possibly threatening the children. Watson believes that something terrifying and occult may be at work. Neither is prepared for the true target of the Napoleonists, or of the Emperor's ghost

The Adventure of the Pinched Palimpsest. A professor has been proselytizing for anarchism. Three students fall for his doctrines and engage in direct action by stealing priceless artifacts from the British Museum, returning them to the oppressed people from whom their colonial masters stole them. In the midst of their caper, a museum guard is shot dead, and they are charged with the murder. After being persuaded by a vulnerable friend of the students, Sherlock Holmes agrees to take on the case. He soon discovers that no one involved is telling the complete truth. Join Holmes and Watson as they race from London to Oxford, then to Cambridge and finally up to a remote village in Scotland and seek to discover the clues that are tied to an obscure medieval palimpsest.

The Adventure of the Missing Better Half. Did you ever wonder what happened to Godfrey Staunton, the missing Three-Quarter, after Holmes found him? This story tells you. He met an exceptional young woman, fell in love, and got married. He was chosen to play on England's National Team in the 1899 Home Nations Championship games. Life was good. ... and then it got much worse. Together -- Godfrey Staunton, Dr. Leslie Armstrong, Dr. Watson, and Sherlock Holmes -- must stop an unspeakable crime taking place. This 38th New Sherlock Holmes. A tribute to *The Adventure of the Missing Three Quarter.*

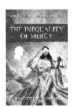

The Inequality of Mercy. What happened after Sherlock Holmes and Dr. Watson pardoned Captain Jack Croker for killing Sir Eustace at the Abbey Grange. Have you imagined that he sailed the seven seas for a year and then returned to his beautiful, beloved Mary Fraser? That didn't happen. A year later, murder, treachery, and international intrigue descended on Abbey Grange, and, once again, Sherlock Holmes was called upon to bring criminals to justice and assist in the course of true love. Buy the story now, and find out what happened.

The Adventure of the Second Entente. In June of 1901, a wealthy young nobleman is murdered, and yet again, Scotland Yard requires help from Sherlock Holmes. The baron has recently returned from an expedition searching for oil in Persia. His only relative and sole heir, a woman from California is the obvious suspect. But then she comes to Sherlock Holmes desperately seeking his help. If she did not kill the man, then who did? Join Holmes, Watson and an unusual woman as they seek to solve the crime and avoid becoming victims themselves. The story is a tribute to the original Sherlock Holmes mystery, *The Adventure of the Second Stain.*

The Adventure of the Morning Glory Murders. Sherlock Holmes confronts the horrible racial and religious prejudice that was rampant in the Victorian era and helps the heroic victims of those evils discover a new life.A family from Argentina has disappeared and it is feared that they were abducted. Their lives are in danger. The father, a colonel in the Argentine army has enemies from years ago that may be seeking revenge. The gigantic 'mulatto' who was the cook in the story about Wisteria Lodge (remember him?) is falsely accused. With his help, Sherlock Holmes must find the family before it is too late.If reading about the prejudices of the Victorian era -- many of which appeared in the original Sherlock Holmes stories -- upsets you, this is not for you. However, if you want to read about how brave people faced those evils and overcame them, this is a story you will enjoy.

www.SherlockHolmesMystery.com

Contributions to
The Great Game of
Sherlockian Scholarship

Sherlock and Barack. This is NOT a new Sherlock Holmes Mystery. It is a Sherlockian research monograph. Why did Barack Obama win in November 2012? Why did Mitt Romney lose? Pundits and political scientists have offered countless reasons. This book reveals the truth - The Sherlock Holmes Factor. Had it not been for Sherlock Holmes, Mitt Romney would be president.

From The Beryl Coronet to Vimy Ridge. This is NOT a New Sherlock Holmes Mystery. It is a monograph of Sherlockian research. This new monograph in the Great Game of Sherlockian scholarship argues that there was a Sherlock Holmes factor in the causes of World War I... and that it is secretly revealed in the *roman a clef* story that we know as *The Adventure of the Beryl Coronet*

www.SherlockHolmesMystery.com

Reverend Ezekiel Black—'The Sherlock Holmes of the American West'—Mystery Stories.

 *A Scarlet Trail of Murder.* At ten o'clock on Sunday morning, the twenty-second of October, 1882, in an abandoned house in the West Bottom of Kansas City, a fellow named Jasper Harrison did not wake up. His inability to do was the result of his having had his throat cut. The Reverend Mr. Ezekiel Black, a part-time Methodist minister, and an itinerant US Marshall is called in. This original western mystery was inspired by the great Sherlock Holmes classic, *A Study in Scarlet*

 *The Brand of the Flying Four.* This case all began one quiet evening in a room in Kansas City. A few weeks later, a gruesome murder, took place in Denver. By the time Rev. Black had solved the mystery, justice, of the frontier variety, not the courtroom, had been meted out.

The story is inspired by *The Sign of the Four* by Arthur Conan Doyle, and like that story, it combines murder most foul, and romance most enticing.

www.SherlockHolmesMystery.com

Collection Sets for eBooks and paperback are available at *40% off the price of buying them separately.*

Collection One
The Sign of the Tooth
The Hudson Valley Mystery
A Case of Identity Theft
The Bald-Headed Trust
Studying Scarlet
The Mystery of the Five Oranges

Collection Two
A Sandal from East Anglia
The Man Who Was Twisted But Hip
The Blue Belt Buckle
The Spectred Bat

Collection Three
The Engineer's Mom
The Notable Bachelorette
The Beryl Anarchists
The Coiffured Bitches

Collection Four

The Silver Horse, Braised
The Box of Cards
The Yellow Farce
The Three Rhodes Not Taken

Collection Five

The Stock Market Murders
The Glorious Yacht
The Most Grave Ritual
The Spy Gate Liars

Collection Six

The Cuckold Man
The Impatient Dissidents
The Grecian, Earned
The Naval Knaves

Collection Seven

The Binomial Asteroid Problem
The Mystery of 222 Baker Street
The Adventure of Charlotte Europa Golderton
The Adventure of the Norwood Rembrandt

Collection Eight

The Dancer from the Dance
The Adventure of the Prioress's Tale
The Adventure of Mrs. J. L. Heber
The Solitary Bicycle Thief

Collection Nine

The Adventure of Charlotte Europa Golderton
The Return of Napoleon
The Adventure of the Pinched Palimpsest
The Adventure of the Missing Better Half

Super Collections A and B

40 New Sherlock Holmes Mysteries.

The perfect ebooks for readers who can only borrow one book a month from Amazon

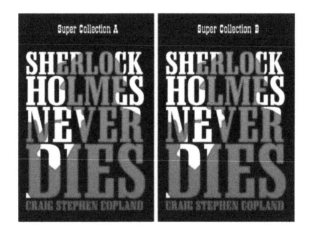

www.SherlockHolmesMystery.com

The Adventure of the Red Circle

The Original Sherlock Holmes Story

Arthur Conan Doyle

The Adventure of the Red Circle

PART I

"Well, Mrs. Warren, I cannot see that you have any particular cause for uneasiness, nor do I understand why I, whose time is of some value, should interfere in the matter. I really have other things to engage me." So spoke Sherlock Holmes and turned back to the great scrapbook in which he was arranging and indexing some of his recent material.

But the landlady had the pertinacity and also the cunning of her sex. She held her ground firmly.

"You arranged an affair for a lodger of mine last year," she said--"Mr. Fairdale Hobbs."

"Ah, yes--a simple matter."

"But he would never cease talking of it--your kindness, sir, and the way in which you brought light into the darkness. I remembered his words when I was in doubt and darkness myself. I know you could if you only would."

Holmes was accessible upon the side of flattery, and also, to do him justice, upon the side of kindliness. The two forces made him lay down his gum-brush with a sigh of resignation and push back his chair.

"Well, well, Mrs. Warren, let us hear about it, then. You don't object to tobacco, I take it? Thank you, Watson--the matches! You are uneasy, as I understand, because your new lodger remains in his rooms and you cannot see him. Why, bless you, Mrs. Warren, if I were your lodger you often would not see me for weeks on end."

"No doubt, sir; but this is different. It frightens me, Mr. Holmes. I can't sleep for fright. To hear his quick step moving here and moving there from early morning to late at night, and yet never to catch so much as a glimpse of him--it's more than I can stand. My husband is as nervous over it as I am, but he is out at his work all day, while I get no rest from it. What is he hiding for? What has he done? Except for the girl, I am all alone in the house with him, and it's more than my nerves can stand."

Holmes leaned forward and laid his long, thin fingers upon the woman's shoulder. He had an almost hypnotic power of soothing when he wished. The scared look faded from her eyes, and her agitated features smoothed into their usual commonplace. She sat down in the chair which he had indicated.

"If I take it up I must understand every detail," said he. "Take time to consider. The smallest point may be the most essential. You say that the man came ten days ago and paid you for a fortnight's board and lodging?"

"He asked my terms, sir. I said fifty shillings a week. There is a small sitting-room and bedroom, and all complete, at the top of the house."

"Well?"

"He said, 'I'll pay you five pounds a week if I can have it on my own terms.' I'm a poor woman, sir, and Mr. Warren earns little, and the money meant much to me. He took out a ten-pound note, and he held it out to me then and there. 'You can have the same every fortnight for a long time to come if you keep the terms,' he said. 'If not, I'll have no more to do with you.'

"What were the terms?"

"Well, sir, they were that he was to have a key of the house. That was all right. Lodgers often have them. Also, that he was to be left entirely to himself and never, upon any excuse, to be disturbed."

"Nothing wonderful in that, surely?"

"Not in reason, sir. But this is out of all reason. He has been there for ten days, and neither Mr. Warren, nor I, nor the girl has once set eyes upon him. We can hear that quick step of his pacing up and down, up and down, night, morning, and noon; but except on that first night he had never once gone out of the house."

"Oh, he went out the first night, did he?"

"Yes, sir, and returned very late--after we were all in bed. He told me after he had taken the rooms that he would do so and asked me not to bar the door. I heard him come up the stair after midnight."

"But his meals?"

"It was his particular direction that we should always, when he rang, leave his meal upon a chair, outside his door. Then he rings again when he has finished, and we take it down from the same chair. If he wants anything else he prints it on a slip of paper and leaves it."

"Prints it?"

"Yes, sir; prints it in pencil. Just the word, nothing more. Here's the one I brought to show you--soap. Here's another--match. This is one he left the first morning--daily gazette. I leave that paper with his breakfast every morning."

"Dear me, Watson," said Homes, staring with great curiosity at the slips of foolscap which the landlady had handed to him, "this is certainly a little unusual. Seclusion I can understand; but why print? Printing is a clumsy process. Why not write? What would it suggest, Watson?"

"That he desired to conceal his handwriting."

"But why? What can it matter to him that his landlady should have a word of his writing? Still, it may be as you say. Then, again, why such laconic messages?"

"I cannot imagine."

"It opens a pleasing field for intelligent speculation. The words are written with a broad-pointed, violet-tinted pencil of a not unusual pattern. You will observe that the paper is torn away at the side here after the printing was done, so that the 's' of 'soap' is partly gone. Suggestive, Watson, is it not?"

"Of caution?"

"Exactly. There was evidently some mark, some thumbprint, something which might give a clue to the person's identity. Now. Mrs. Warren, you say that the man was of middle size, dark, and bearded. What age would he be?"

"Youngish, sir--not over thirty."

"Well, can you give me no further indications?"

"He spoke good English, sir, and yet I thought he was a foreigner by his accent."

"And he was well dressed?"

"Very smartly dressed, sir--quite the gentleman. Dark clothes--nothing you would note."

"He gave no name?"

"No, sir."

"And has had no letters or callers?"

"None."

"But surely you or the girl enter his room of a morning?"

"No, sir; he looks after himself entirely."

"Dear me! that is certainly remarkable. What about his luggage?"

"He had one big brown bag with him--nothing else."

"Well, we don't seem to have much material to help us. Do you say nothing has come out of that room--absolutely nothing?"

The landlady drew an envelope from her bag; from it she shook out two burnt matches and a cigarette-end upon the table.

"They were on his tray this morning. I brought them because I had heard that you can read great things out of small ones."

Holmes shrugged his shoulders.

"There is nothing here," said he. "The matches have, of course, been used to light cigarettes. That is obvious from the shortness of the burnt end. Half the match is consumed in lighting a pipe or cigar. But, dear me! this cigarette stub is certainly remarkable. The gentleman was bearded and moustached, you say?"

"Yes, sir."

"I don't understand that. I should say that only a clean-shaven man could have smoked this. Why, Watson, even your modest moustache would have been singed."

"A holder?" I suggested.

"No, no; the end is matted. I suppose there could not be two people in your rooms, Mrs. Warren?"

"No, sir. He eats so little that I often wonder it can keep life in one."

"Well, I think we must wait for a little more material. After all, you have nothing to complain of. You have received your rent, and he is not a troublesome lodger, though he is certainly an unusual one. He pays you well, and if he chooses to lie concealed it is no direct business of yours. We have no excuse for an intrusion upon his privacy until we have some reason to think that there is a guilty reason for it. I've taken up the matter, and I won't lose sight of it. Report to me if anything fresh occurs, and rely upon my assistance if it should be needed.

"There are certainly some points of interest in this case, Watson," he remarked when the landlady had left us. "It may, of course, be trivial--individual eccentricity; or it may be very much deeper than appears on the surface. The first thing that strikes one is the obvious possibility that the person now in the rooms may be entirely different from the one who engaged them."

"Why should you think so?"

"Well, apart from this cigarette-end, was it not suggestive that the only time the lodger went out was immediately after his taking the rooms? He came back--or someone came back--when all witnesses were out of the way. We have no proof that the person who came back was the person who went out. Then, again, the man who took the rooms spoke English well. This other, however, prints 'match' when it should have been 'matches.' I can imagine that the word was taken out of a dictionary, which would give the noun but not the plural. The laconic style may be to conceal the absence of knowledge of English. Yes, Watson, there are good reasons to suspect that there has been a substitution of lodgers."

"But for what possible end?"

"Ah! there lies our problem. There is one rather obvious line of investigation." He took down the great book in which, day by day, he filed the agony columns of the various London journals. "Dear me!" said he, turning over the pages, "what a chorus of groans, cries, and bleatings! What a rag-bag of singular happenings! But surely the most valuable hunting-ground that ever was given to a student of the unusual! This person is alone and cannot be approached by letter without a breach of that absolute secrecy which is desired. How is any news or any message to reach him from without? Obviously by advertisement through a newspaper. There seems no other way, and fortunately we need concern ourselves with the one paper only. Here are the Daily Gazette extracts of the last fortnight. 'Lady with a black boa at Prince's Skating Club'--that we may pass. 'Surely Jimmy will not break his mother's heart'--that appears to be irrelevant. 'If the lady who fainted on Brixton bus'--she does not interest me. 'Every day my heart longs--' Bleat, Watson-- unmitigated bleat! Ah, this is a little more possible. Listen to this: 'Be patient. Will find some sure means of communications. Meanwhile, this column. G.' That is two days after Mrs. Warren's lodger arrived. It sounds plausible, does it not? The mysterious one could understand English, even if he could not print it. Let us see if we can pick up the trace again. Yes, here we are--three days later. 'Am making successful arrangements. Patience and prudence. The clouds will pass. G.' Nothing for a week after that. Then comes something much more definite: 'The path is clearing. If I find chance signal message remember code agreed--One A, two B, and so on. You will hear soon. G.' That was in yesterday's paper, and there is nothing in to-day's. It's all very appropriate to Mrs. Warren's lodger. If we wait a little, Watson, I don't doubt that the affair will grow more intelligible."

So it proved; for in the morning I found my friend standing on the hearthrug with his back to the fire and a smile of complete satisfaction upon his face.

"How's this, Watson?" he cried, picking up the paper from the table. "'High red house with white stone facings. Third floor. Second window left. After dusk. G.' That is definite enough. I think after breakfast we must make a little reconnaissance of Mrs. Warren's neighbourhood. Ah, Mrs. Warren! what news do you bring us this morning?"

Our client had suddenly burst into the room with an explosive energy which told of some new and momentous development.

"It's a police matter, Mr. Holmes!" she cried. "I'll have no more of it! He shall pack out of there with his baggage. I would have gone straight up and told him so, only I thought it was but fair to you to take your opinion first. But I'm at the end of my patience, and when it comes to knocking my old man about--"

"Knocking Mr. Warren about?"

"Using him roughly, anyway."

"But who used him roughly?"

"Ah! that's what we want to know! It was this morning, sir. Mr. Warren is a timekeeper at Morton and Waylight's, in Tottenham Court Road. He has to be out of the house before seven. Well, this morning he had not gone ten paces down the road when two men came up behind him, threw a coat over his head, and bundled him into a cab that was beside the curb. They drove him an hour, and then opened the door and shot him out. He lay in the roadway so shaken in his wits that he never saw what became of the cab. When he picked himself up he found he was on Hampstead Heath; so he took a bus home, and there he lies now on his sofa, while I came straight round to tell you what had happened."

"Most interesting," said Holmes. "Did he observe the appearance of these men--did he hear them talk?"

"No; he is clean dazed. He just knows that he was lifted up as if by magic and dropped as if by magic. Two at least were in it, and maybe three."

"And you connect this attack with your lodger?"

"Well, we've lived there fifteen years and no such happenings ever came before. I've had enough of him. Money's not everything. I'll have him out of my house before the day is done."

"Wait a bit, Mrs. Warren. Do nothing rash. I begin to think that this affair may be very much more important than appeared at first sight. It is clear now that some danger is threatening your lodger. It is equally clear that his enemies, lying in wait for him near your door, mistook your husband for him in the foggy morning light. On discovering their mistake they released him. What they would have done had it not been a mistake, we can only conjecture."

"Well, what am I to do, Mr. Holmes?"

"I have a great fancy to see this lodger of yours, Mrs. Warren."

"I don't see how that is to be managed, unless you break in the door. I always hear him unlock it as I go down the stair after I leave the tray."

"He has to take the tray in. Surely we could conceal ourselves and see him do it."

The landlady thought for a moment.

"Well, sir, there's the box-room opposite. I could arrange a looking-glass, maybe, and if you were behind the door--"

"Excellent!" said Holmes. "When does he lunch?"

"About one, sir."

"Then Dr. Watson and I will come round in time. For the present, Mrs. Warren, good-bye."

At half-past twelve we found ourselves upon the steps of Mrs. Warren's house--a high, thin, yellow-brick edifice in Great Orme Street, a narrow thoroughfare at the northeast side of the British Museum. Standing as it does near the corner of the street, it commands a view down Howe Street, with its more pretentious houses. Holmes pointed with a chuckle to one of these, a row of residential flats, which projected so that they could not fail to catch the eye.

"See, Watson!" said he. "'High red house with stone facings.' There is the signal station all right. We know the place, and we know the code; so surely our task should be simple. There's a 'to let' card in that window. It is evidently an empty flat to which the confederate has access. Well, Mrs. Warren, what now?"

"I have it all ready for you. If you will both come up and leave your boots below on the landing, I'll put you there now."

It was an excellent hiding-place which she had arranged. The mirror was so placed that, seated in the dark, we could very plainly see the door opposite. We had hardly settled down in it, and Mrs. Warren left us, when a distant tinkle announced that our mysterious neighbour had rung. Presently the landlady appeared with the tray, laid it down upon a chair beside the closed door, and then, treading heavily, departed. Crouching together in the angle of the door, we kept our eyes fixed upon the mirror. Suddenly, as the landlady's footsteps died away, there was the creak of a turning key, the handle revolved, and two thin hands darted out and lifted the tray from the chair. An instant later it was hurriedly replaced, and I caught a glimpse of a dark, beautiful, horrified face glaring at the narrow opening of the box-room. Then the door crashed to, the key turned once more, and all was silence. Holmes twitched my sleeve, and together we stole down the stair.

"I will call again in the evening," said he to the expectant landlady. "I think, Watson, we can discuss this business better in our own quarters."

"My surmise, as you saw, proved to be correct," said he, speaking from the depths of his easy-chair. "There has been a substitution of lodgers. What I did not foresee is that we should find a woman, and no ordinary woman, Watson."

"She saw us."

"Well, she saw something to alarm her. That is certain. The general sequence of events is pretty clear, is it not? A couple seek refuge in London from a very terrible and instant danger. The measure of that danger is the rigour of their precautions. The man, who has some work which he must do, desires to leave the woman in absolute safety while he does it. It is not an easy problem, but he solved it in an original fashion, and so effectively that her presence was not even known to the landlady who supplies her with food. The printed messages, as is now evident, were to prevent her sex being discovered by her writing. The man cannot come near the woman, or he will guide their enemies to her. Since he cannot communicate with her direct, he has recourse to the agony column of a paper. So far all is clear."

"But what is at the root of it?"

"Ah, yes, Watson--severely practical, as usual! What is at the root of it all? Mrs. Warren's whimsical problem enlarges somewhat and assumes a more sinister aspect as we proceed. This much we can say: that it is no ordinary love escapade. You saw the woman's face at the sign of danger. We have heard, too, of the attack upon the landlord, which was undoubtedly meant for the lodger. These alarms, and the desperate need for secrecy, argue that the matter is one of life or death. The attack upon Mr. Warren further shows that the enemy, whoever they are, are themselves not aware of the substitution of the female lodger for the male. It is very curious and complex, Watson."

"Why should you go further in it? What have you to gain from it?"

"What, indeed? It is art for art's sake, Watson. I suppose when you doctored you found yourself studying cases without thought of a fee?"

"For my education, Holmes."

"Education never ends, Watson. It is a series of lessons with the greatest for the last. This is an instructive case. There is neither money nor credit in it, and yet one would wish to tidy it up. When dusk comes we should find ourselves one stage advanced in our investigation."

When we returned to Mrs. Warren's rooms, the gloom of a London winter evening had thickened into one gray curtain, a dead monotone of colour, broken only by the sharp yellow squares of the windows and the blurred haloes of the gas-lamps. As we peered from the darkened sitting-room of the lodging-house, one more dim light glimmered high up through the obscurity.

"Someone is moving in that room," said Holmes in a whisper, his gaunt and eager face thrust forward to the window-pane. "Yes, I can see his shadow. There he is again! He has a candle in his hand. Now he is peering across. He wants to be sure that she is on the lookout. Now he begins to flash. Take the message also, Watson, that we may check each other. A single flash--that is A, surely. Now, then. How many did you make it? Twenty. So did I. That should mean T. AT--that's intelligible enough. Another T. Surely this is the beginning of a second word. Now, then--TENTA. Dead stop. That can't be all, Watson? ATTENTA gives no sense. Nor is it any better as three words AT, TEN, TA, unless T. A. are a person's initials. There it goes again! What's that? ATTE--why, it is the same message over again. Curious, Watson, very curious. Now he is off once more! AT--why he is repeating it for the third time. ATTENTA three times! How often will he repeat it? No, that seems to be the finish. He has withdrawn from the window. What do you make of it, Watson?"

"A cipher message, Holmes."

My companion gave a sudden chuckle of comprehension. "And not a very obscure cipher, Watson," said he. "Why, of course, it is Italian! The A means that it is addressed to a woman. 'Beware! Beware! Beware!' How's that, Watson?

"I believe you have hit it."

"Not a doubt of it. It is a very urgent message, thrice repeated to make it more so. But beware of what? Wait a bit, he is coming to the window once more."

Again we saw the dim silhouette of a crouching man and the whisk of the small flame across the window as the signals were renewed. They came more rapidly than before--so rapid that it was hard to follow them.

"PERICOLO--pericolo--eh, what's that, Watson? 'Danger,' isn't it? Yes, by Jove, it's a danger signal. There he goes again! PERI. Halloa, what on earth--"

The light had suddenly gone out, the glimmering square of window had disappeared, and the third floor formed a dark band round the lofty building, with its tiers of shining casements. That last warning cry had been suddenly cut short. How, and by whom? The same thought occurred on the instant to us both. Holmes sprang up from where he crouched by the window.

"This is serious, Watson," he cried. "There is some devilry going forward! Why should such a message stop in such a way? I should put Scotland Yard in touch with this business--and yet, it is too pressing for us to leave."

"Shall I go for the police?"

"We must define the situation a little more clearly. It may bear some more innocent interpretation. Come, Watson, let us go across ourselves and see what we can make of it."

PART II

As we walked rapidly down Howe Street I glanced back at the building which we had left. There, dimly outlined at the top window, I could see the shadow of a head, a woman's head, gazing tensely, rigidly, out into the night, waiting with breathless suspense for the renewal of that interrupted message. At the doorway of the Howe Street flats a man, muffled in a cravat and greatcoat, was leaning against the railing. He started as the hall-light fell upon our faces.

"Holmes!" he cried.

"Why, Gregson!" said my companion as he shook hands with the Scotland Yard detective. "Journeys end with lovers' meetings. What brings you here?"

"The same reasons that bring you, I expect," said Gregson. "How you got on to it I can't imagine."

"Different threads, but leading up to the same tangle. I've been taking the signals."

"Signals?"

"Yes, from that window. They broke off in the middle. We came over to see the reason. But since it is safe in your hands I see no object in continuing this business."

"Wait a bit!" cried Gregson eagerly. "I'll do you this justice, Mr. Holmes, that I was never in a case yet that I didn't feel stronger for having you on my side. There's only the one exit to these flats, so we have him safe."

"Who is he?"

"Well, well, we score over you for once, Mr. Holmes. You must give us best this time." He struck his stick sharply upon the ground, on which a cabman, his whip in his hand, sauntered over from a four-wheeler which stood on the far side of the street. "May I introduce you to Mr. Sherlock Holmes?" he said to the cabman. "This is Mr. Leverton, of Pinkerton's American Agency."

"The hero of the Long Island cave mystery?" said Holmes. "Sir, I am pleased to meet you."

The American, a quiet, businesslike young man, with a clean-shaven, hatchet face, flushed up at the words of commendation. "I am on the trail of my life now, Mr. Holmes," said he. "If I can get Gorgiano--"

"What! Gorgiano of the Red Circle?"

"Oh, he has a European fame, has he? Well, we've learned all about him in America. We KNOW he is at the bottom of fifty murders, and yet we have nothing positive we can take him on. I tracked him over from New York, and I've been close to him for a week in London, waiting some excuse to get my hand on his collar. Mr. Gregson and I ran him to ground in that big tenement house, and there's only one door, so he can't slip us. There's three folk come out since he went in, but I'll swear he wasn't one of them."

"Mr. Holmes talks of signals," said Gregson. "I expect, as usual, he knows a good deal that we don't."

In a few clear words Holmes explained the situation as it had appeared to us. The American struck his hands together with vexation.

"He's on to us!" he cried.

"Why do you think so?"

"Well, it figures out that way, does it not? Here he is, sending out messages to an accomplice--there are several of his gang in London. Then suddenly, just as by your own account he was telling them that there was danger, he broke short off. What could it mean except that from the window he had suddenly either caught sight of us in the street, or in some way come to understand how close the danger was, and that he must act right away if he was to avoid it? What do you suggest, Mr. Holmes?"

"That we go up at once and see for ourselves."

"But we have no warrant for his arrest."

"He is in unoccupied premises under suspicious circumstances," said Gregson. "That is good enough for the moment. When we have him by the heels we can see if New York can't help us to keep him. I'll take the responsibility of arresting him now."

Our official detectives may blunder in the matter of intelligence, but never in that of courage. Gregson climbed the stair to arrest this desperate murderer with the same absolutely quiet and businesslike bearing with which he would have ascended the official staircase of Scotland Yard. The Pinkerton man had tried to push past him, but Gregson had firmly elbowed him back. London dangers were the privilege of the London force.

The door of the left-hand flat upon the third landing was standing ajar. Gregson pushed it open. Within all was absolute silence and darkness. I struck a match and lit the detective's lantern. As I did so, and as the flicker steadied into a flame, we all gave a gasp of surprise. On the deal boards of the carpetless floor there was outlined a fresh track of blood. The red steps pointed towards us and led away from an inner room, the door of which was closed. Gregson flung it open and held his light full blaze in front of him, while we all peered eagerly over his shoulders.

In the middle of the floor of the empty room was huddled the figure of an enormous man, his clean-shaven, swarthy face grotesquely horrible in its contortion and his head encircled by a ghastly crimson halo of blood, lying in a broad wet circle upon the white woodwork. His knees were drawn up, his hands thrown out in agony, and from the centre of his broad, brown, upturned throat there projected the white haft of a knife driven blade-deep into his body. Giant as he was, the man must have gone down like a poleaxed ox before that terrific blow. Beside his right hand a most formidable horn-handled, two-edged dagger lay upon the floor, and near it a black kid glove.

"By George! it's Black Gorgiano himself!" cried the American detective. "Someone has got ahead of us this time."

"Here is the candle in the window, Mr. Holmes," said Gregson. "Why, whatever are you doing?"

Holmes had stepped across, had lit the candle, and was passing it backward and forward across the window-panes. Then he peered into the darkness, blew the candle out, and threw it on the floor.

"I rather think that will be helpful," said he. He came over and stood in deep thought while the two professionals were examining the body. "You say that three people came out from the flat while you were waiting downstairs," said he at last. "Did you observe them closely?"

"Yes, I did."

"Was there a fellow about thirty, black-bearded, dark, of middle size?"

"Yes; he was the last to pass me."

"That is your man, I fancy. I can give you his description, and we have a very excellent outline of his footmark. That should be enough for you."

"Not much, Mr. Holmes, among the millions of London."

"Perhaps not. That is why I thought it best to summon this lady to your aid."

We all turned round at the words. There, framed in the doorway, was a tall and beautiful woman--the mysterious lodger of Bloomsbury. Slowly she advanced, her face pale and drawn with a frightful apprehension, her eyes fixed and staring, her terrified gaze riveted upon the dark figure on the floor.

"You have killed him!" she muttered. "Oh, Dio mio, you have killed him!" Then I heard a sudden sharp intake of her breath, and she sprang into the air with a cry of joy. Round and round the room she danced, her hands clapping, her dark eyes gleaming with delighted wonder, and a thousand pretty Italian exclamations pouring from her lips. It was terrible and amazing to see such a woman so convulsed with joy at such a sight. Suddenly she stopped and gazed at us all with a questioning stare.

"But you! You are police, are you not? You have killed Giuseppe Gorgiano. Is it not so?"

"We are police, madam."

She looked round into the shadows of the room.

"But where, then, is Gennaro?" she asked. "He is my husband, Gennaro Lucca. I am Emilia Lucca, and we are both from New York. Where is Gennaro? He called me this moment from this window, and I ran with all my speed."

"It was I who called," said Holmes.

"You! How could you call?"

"Your cipher was not difficult, madam. Your presence here was desirable. I knew that I had only to flash 'Vieni' and you would surely come."

The beautiful Italian looked with awe at my companion.

"I do not understand how you know these things," she said. "Giuseppe Gorgiano--how did he--" She paused, and then suddenly her face lit up with pride and delight. "Now I see it! My Gennaro! My splendid, beautiful Gennaro, who has guarded me safe from all harm, he did it, with his own strong hand he killed the monster! Oh, Gennaro, how wonderful you are! What woman could ever be worthy of such a man?"

"Well, Mrs. Lucca," said the prosaic Gregson, laying his hand upon the lady's sleeve with as little sentiment as if she were a Notting Hill hooligan, "I am not very clear yet who you are or what you are; but you've said enough to make it very clear that we shall want you at the Yard."

"One moment, Gregson," said Holmes. "I rather fancy that this lady may be as anxious to give us information as we can be to get it.

You understand, madam, that your husband will be arrested and tried for the death of the man who lies before us? What you say may be used in evidence. But if you think that he has acted from motives which are not criminal, and which he would wish to have known, then you cannot serve him better than by telling us the whole story."

"Now that Gorgiano is dead we fear nothing," said the lady. "He was a devil and a monster, and there can be no judge in the world who would punish my husband for having killed him."

"In that case," said Holmes, "my suggestion is that we lock this door, leave things as we found them, go with this lady to her room, and form our opinion after we have heard what it is that she has to say to us."

Half an hour later we were seated, all four, in the small sitting-room of Signora Lucca, listening to her remarkable narrative of those sinister events, the ending of which we had chanced to witness. She spoke in rapid and fluent but very unconventional English, which, for the sake of clearness, I will make grammatical.

"I was born in Posilippo, near Naples," said she, "and was the daughter of Augusto Barelli, who was the chief lawyer and once the deputy of that part. Gennaro was in my father's employment, and I came to love him, as any woman must. He had neither money nor position--nothing but his beauty and strength and energy--so my father forbade the match. We fled together, were married at Bari, and sold my jewels to gain the money which would take us to America. This was four years ago, and we have been in New York ever since.

"Fortune was very good to us at first. Gennaro was able to do a service to an Italian gentleman--he saved him from some ruffians in the place called the Bowery, and so made a powerful friend. His name was Tito Castalotte, and he was the senior partner of the great firm of Castalotte and Zamba, who are the chief fruit importers of New York. Signor Zamba is an invalid, and our new friend Castalotte has all power within the firm, which employs more than three hundred men. He took my husband into his employment, made him head of a department, and showed his good-will towards him in every way. Signor Castalotte was a bachelor, and I believe that he felt as if Gennaro was his son, and both my husband and I loved him as if he were our father. We had taken and furnished a little house in Brooklyn, and our whole future seemed assured when that black cloud appeared which was soon to overspread our sky.

"One night, when Gennaro returned from his work, he brought a fellow-countryman back with him. His name was Gorgiano, and he had come also from Posilippo. He was a huge man, as you can testify, for you have looked upon his corpse. Not only was his body that of a giant but everything about him was grotesque, gigantic, and terrifying. His voice was like thunder in our little house. There was scarce room for the whirl of his great arms as he talked. His thoughts, his emotions, his passions, all were exaggerated and monstrous. He talked, or rather roared, with such energy that others could but sit and listen, cowed with the mighty stream of words. His eyes blazed at you and held you at his mercy. He was a terrible and wonderful man. I thank God that he is dead!

"He came again and again. Yet I was aware that Gennaro was no more happy than I was in his presence. My poor husband would sit pale and listless, listening to the endless raving upon politics and upon social questions which made up our visitor's conversation. Gennaro said nothing, but I, who knew him so well, could read in his face some emotion which I had never seen there before. At first I thought that it was dislike. And then, gradually, I understood that it was more than dislike. It was fear--a deep, secret, shrinking fear. That night--the night that I read his terror--I put my arms round him and I implored him by his love for me and by all that he held dear to hold nothing from me, and to tell me why this huge man overshadowed him so.

"He told me, and my own heart grew cold as ice as I listened. My poor Gennaro, in his wild and fiery days, when all the world seemed against him and his mind was driven half mad by the injustices of life, had joined a Neapolitan society, the Red Circle, which was allied to the old Carbonari. The oaths and secrets of this brotherhood were frightful, but once within its rule no escape was possible. When we had fled to America Gennaro thought that he had cast it all off forever. What was his horror one evening to meet in the streets the very man who had initiated him in Naples, the giant Gorgiano, a man who had earned the name of 'Death' in the south of Italy, for he was red to the elbow in murder! He had come to New York to avoid the Italian police, and he had already planted a branch of this dreadful society in his new home. All this Gennaro told me and showed me a summons which he had received that very day, a Red Circle drawn upon the head of it telling him that a lodge would be held upon a certain date, and that his presence at it was required and ordered.

"That was bad enough, but worse was to come. I had noticed for some time that when Gorgiano came to us, as he constantly did, in the evening, he spoke much to me; and even when his words were to my husband those terrible, glaring, wild-beast eyes of his were always turned upon me. One night his secret came out. I had awakened what he called 'love' within him--the love of a brute--a savage. Gennaro had not yet returned when he came. He pushed his way in, seized me in his mighty arms, hugged me in his bear's embrace, covered me with kisses, and implored me to come away with him. I was struggling and screaming when Gennaro entered and attacked him. He struck Gennaro senseless and fled from the house which he was never more to enter. It was a deadly enemy that we made that night.

"A few days later came the meeting. Gennaro returned from it with a face which told me that something dreadful had occurred. It was worse than we could have imagined possible. The funds of the society were raised by blackmailing rich Italians and threatening them with violence should they refuse the money. It seems that Castalotte, our dear friend and benefactor, had been approached. He had refused to yield to threats, and he had handed the notices to the police. It was resolved now that such an example should be made of them as would prevent any other victim from rebelling. At the meeting it was arranged that he and his house should be blown up with dynamite. There was a drawing of lots as to who should carry out the deed. Gennaro saw our enemy's cruel face smiling at him as he dipped his hand in the bag. No doubt it had been prearranged in some fashion, for it was the fatal disc with the Red Circle upon it, the mandate for murder, which lay upon his palm. He was to kill his best friend, or he was to expose himself and me to the vengeance of his comrades. It was part of their fiendish system to punish those whom they feared or hated by injuring not only their own persons but those whom they loved, and it was the knowledge of this which hung as a terror over my poor Gennaro's head and drove him nearly crazy with apprehension.

"All that night we sat together, our arms round each other, each strengthening each for the troubles that lay before us. The very next evening had been fixed for the attempt. By midday my husband and I were on our way to London, but not before he had given our benefactor full warning of this danger, and had also left such information for the police as would safeguard his life for the future.

"The rest, gentlemen, you know for yourselves. We were sure that our enemies would be behind us like our own shadows. Gorgiano had his private reasons for vengeance, but in any case we knew how ruthless, cunning, and untiring he could be. Both Italy and America are full of stories of his dreadful powers. If ever they were exerted it would be now. My darling made use of the few clear days which our start had given us in arranging for a refuge for me in such a fashion that no possible danger could reach me. For his own part, he wished to be free that he might communicate both with the American and with the Italian police. I do not myself know where he lived, or how. All that I learned was through the columns of a newspaper. But once as I looked through my window, I saw two Italians watching the house, and I understood that in some way Gorgiano had found our retreat. Finally Gennaro told me, through the paper, that he would signal to me from a certain window, but when the signals came they were nothing but warnings, which were suddenly interrupted. It is very clear to me now that he knew

Gorgiano to be close upon him, and that, thank God! he was ready for him when he came. And now, gentleman, I would ask you whether we have anything to fear from the law, or whether any judge upon earth would condemn my Gennaro for what he has done?"

"Well, Mr. Gregson," said the American, looking across at the official, "I don't know what your British point of view may be, but I guess that in New York this lady's husband will receive a pretty general vote of thanks."

"She will have to come with me and see the chief," Gregson answered. "If what she says is corroborated, I do not think she or her husband has much to fear. But what I can't make head or tail of, Mr. Holmes, is how on earth YOU got yourself mixed up in the matter."

"Education, Gregson, education. Still seeking knowledge at the old university. Well, Watson, you have one more specimen of the tragic and grotesque to add to your collection. By the way, it is not eight o'clock, and a Wagner night at Covent Garden! If we hurry, we might be in time for the second act."

Made in the USA
Las Vegas, NV
04 March 2021